Seeker of the Gentle Heart

Seeker of the Gentle Heart

Blaine M. Yorgason and Brenton G. Yorgason

Bookcraft • Salt Lake City, Utah

Library of Congress Catalog Card Number: 82-70692
ISBN 0-88494-456-5

2 3 4 5 6 7 8 9 10   89 88 87 86 85 84 83 82

Lithographed in the United States of America
PUBLISHERS PRESS
Salt Lake City, Utah

For Don, Jim, and Milt,
who first challenged
and then lifted
our thinking

Authors' Note

Seeker of the Gentle Heart, a story of members of an eastern Iroquoian tribe of American Indians known as the Susquehannocks, is the second in a three-part series dealing, through the lives and attitudes of native Americans, with questions which seem to trouble most of mankind. The first volume, *The Windwalker*, examined man's relationship with himself, with his God, and with his family. This volume concerns itself more with man's relationship and responsibilities to all others.

The historical incidents reported in the story are fundamentally accurate and occurred when and where stated. Likewise, the attitudes and philosophies, including man/woman relationships, attributed to the principal characters, and by inference to their corresponding races, are also historical. Seventeenth-, eighteenth- and nineteenth-century Americans, both red and white, recorded their attitudes and philosophies in their oral traditions, books, journals, and private papers. These are readily available for study today and have been used extensively in preparing this book.

The characters of Andaggy, Malcom O'Connor, Hairy Man, Sheehays, and Kyunqueagoah (Stone Flower, Milly) are fictional, and are based only incidentally upon a composite of historical persons and incidents. The Indian names themselves are Susquehannock in origin.

Many of Milly's statements concerning peace and Indian/White relationships have been developed from the recorded statements of Indians of that period. For the purposes of this story, these statements have been modified and credited to her.

The pale god in the story is a being spoken of in legends found throughout the Americas. In the legends he appears mysteriously about two thousand years ago, teaches his peace religion to the people, and then vanishes just as mysteriously. Though the actual identity of this fascinating personage is not established in Indian lore, there is no doubt concerning the tremendous impact of his

teachings and message. It is our intention, as authors, to explore
his activities more thoroughly in an upcoming volume, the third in
the above-mentioned series, entitled *Circles of the Dawn*.

Contents

Prologue

A dark curtain of rain swept across the black and choppy waters of the bay, hiding the few dim lights on the distant shore and whipping the white-capped waves into frenzied hissing. High on the forecastle of a darkened ship the figure of a man sat hunched against the deck railing, patiently waiting. In the darkness he was nearly invisible, and when the rain finally scudded against the timbers of the ship, sweeping over him, he became almost totally so.

At first the man gave no sign that he noticed the rain, but at last he shrugged his shoulders slightly and pulled his sealskin coat more tightly around his neck. Then, as he had done several times in the past few minutes, he inched himself up to where he could see the water below. Carefully he looked down into the darkness, but there was still no movement, no sign of the tiny craft which was to spirit him away from his floating prison.

Easing back down, he began methodically to massage his leg, a leg that was becoming increasingly troublesome. The ship's doctor had insisted time and again that it was only bruised and that, given time, the bruise would work itself out. But it was no bruise, and the man knew it. It was the gout, and it was caused by nothing but the passing of the years and the constant exposure to the vagaries of the weather. So he massaged the leg and he waited, patient and yet driven to impatience by the danger of his position, the urgency of his mission, and the pain in his leg.

Malcom O'Connor, he said softly to himself, *are you thinking more of your pain than of your escape? That's not a good thing, man, and you'd better be more alert. Aye, and that especially with the first mate apt to be prowling about.*

Cautiously the man named Malcom O'Connor eased himself into a more comfortable position, wedging his aching body deeper between the railing and the coils of hemp rope which had been stacked nearby. Down on the deck amidships the timbers creaked where a sentry prowled, and now and again O'Connor caught a glimmering of light from the man's rain-drenched clothing.

Though he did not fear the sentry, neither did O'Connor treat the man's presence lightly. One sentry could bring the entire ship to battle stations within minutes, and several crack British gunners would have little difficulty in bringing to an early conclusion his hastily planned escape. That must not happen, and he knew it. Nor would it, if it was in his power to avoid detection.

Nor was it only himself he was thinking of, though that might have been true in years past. Now, however, he hoped he was beyond such selfishness. Now his escape and his actions could affect the peoples of at least three nations, and perhaps twice or three times that many more. The message he carried, the message he must deliver just four days hence to the one who was called The Builder, was so vital that he doubted even his own comprehension of it. Yet a glimmering of understanding was with him, and that glimmering gave him a patience and an endurance which were not normally his.

Above him the wind from the spring squall whistled wildly through the rigging. Listening, doing his best to blank his mind against the pain in his leg, Malcom O'Connor thought of what he was about to do. Even though his impressment into British service had been illegal, his desertion from the ship would be considered just as much so. It would even, were he by some chance captured, result in his execution. So why, he asked himself, was he attempting to escape?

Again he pulled himself to his feet, again he saw nothing, and again he crouched back down against the railing, still waiting.

He thought then of the person he hoped to meet, the one who was called The Builder. Actually, he knew little enough of him. Yet what he did know—his ability with words, his great courage, and his strong stand for peace—were enough to convince Malcom O'Connor that the two must meet.

In addition, there were two other reasons which compelled Malcom O'Connor to desire an immediate meeting. The first was a strange dream he had had recently, in which he had seen one who was called The Builder. That in itself had been unusual, but it was not sufficient reason for him to risk his life. The second reason, the one of most significance, had come a fortnight past, when a man, an almost forgotten friend of his youth, had come with his son to deliver supplies to the ship. As the two men recognized each other and became reacquainted, their conversation turned to memories of western New York State and to events that had filled their lives as young men.

Later, as the man and his boy were preparing to disembark, the man chanced to mention that at least one person from Donegal Springs, which he remembered had been Malcom's first home, had gained some renown. To O'Connor's question as to who it was, the man gave the name of the one who was known as The Builder.

Now, as Malcom O'Connor sat shivering in the cold night rain, he recalled the strange excitement he had felt at his friend's disclosure. The Builder was not only one who felt as he did about peace but one who came from the same area as he did. Because of that, he could no doubt answer many of the questions which had troubled Malcom O'Connor throughout his life, questions concerning his own clouded past.

With the years speeding by so relentlessly, his confusion about his identity was bothering him greatly. Why, for instance, did he always feel alone? Or why was he always so concerned about goodwill between men? Why did he feel things that others around him never seemed to feel? If he knew who he was, he reasoned, if he knew of his parents and of his family, then such questions could easily be answered, and he would be at peace. Somehow he felt—or perhaps it was only a hope— that the one known as The Builder could help him.

He had therefore given quick instructions to his old friend, who agreed instantly to act as a courier and an accomplice. Time had slipped by, and word had come to him two days ago that the hoped-for meeting had been arranged. The Builder was coming to the valley of the Susquehanna six days from then and would meet him on the point of land above the mouth of Conewago Creek shortly after sunrise.

O'Connor had arranged his escape as quickly as possible, and now he waited impatiently in the driving rain, knowing that four days was almost not enough time, worrying lest his escape had been poorly timed and ill-planned, distraught because his leg was such a hindrance.

There came a sudden but very slight bump against the side of the ship. Rising, O'Connor saw the brief wink of a hooded lantern below him, bright against the blackness of the water, and he was ready.

Instantly the rope was in his hand, snaking over the side and into the darkness below. For a moment then he waited, holding his breath, but at last there was a slight tug and he knew that all was secure.

Quickly and silently he took hold of his bad leg with both hands and lifted it so that he could get it over the railing. Then, gritting his teeth against the pain, he prepared for his next move.

"Are ye leaving us so soon, Mr. O'Connor?" The voice came from the blackness behind him.

Malcom O'Connor, frozen into immobility by the icily sarcastic question of the first mate, stood with his leg propped on the railing of the British sloop, in about as helpless a position as he had ever been. How had the man known he was there, he wondered frantically? Had the mate's discovery been by chance, or did the entire ship know of his plans?

There was no way of knowing, of course, but neither did it actually matter. He must behave as though the mate were alone, and then take the consequences if that should prove incorrect. Nor would the mate expect what O'Connor planned to do, for in the man's mind Malcom O'Connor was a coward, pure and simple. To the mate, who was a brute of a man, the impressed American sailor was simply an old fool, someone to be mocked and ridiculed, but never one to be feared.

Without hesitating, without wasting time with speech, and with all the strength his husky old body could muster, O'Connor pivoted on his one leg, in the same movement swinging his clenched fist in a powerful swing that landed squarely against the side of the startled mate's jaw. Apart from the sodden crunch of bone against bone there was no sound, not even when the mate collapsed onto the rope which had been piled upon the deck.

Quickly O'Connor knelt beside the fallen man, fearful that he had killed him. But that was not the case, for though his jaw was shattered terribly, the mate's breathing was regular and deep. He would recover.

"I'm sorry, Mr. Quinn," O'Connor whispered quietly. "I truly am. Though you mightily deserved this, it would not be my way. As I have told you before, I am a man of peace, and wish hurt upon no man. Nevertheless, perhaps the crew will enjoy my unplanned gift to them, the gift of your silence. For you will be silent, Mr. Quinn. You will be silent, methinks, for some time to come."

Rising quietly, the man called Malcom O'Connor stepped to the side of the ship, took hold of the rope, slipped over the side, and handed himself down to the dinghy which waited below. Once he was seated, his childhood friend nodded to his son, who nodded back and then silently dipped his oars into the black waters of the bay. Within seconds the small craft and its three occupants were gone into the darkness of the storm.

The mission, the search for the peace of identity, had begun.

The Meeting

I espied the man initially when he was still far up the River Sus-quehanna, coming toward me. At first I was not certain, for he was very nearly hidden in the shadows along the tree-lined shore. Although there were not likely to be enemies about, he was taking no chances, none at all. Before each stretch of open water he paused, paddle in hand, while he looked carefully around. Nor did he paddle into the warm sunlight that was creeping toward him across the water. He stayed always where he was obscured by shadow, preferring the safety there to the danger which would be his were he more comfortable.

It was the year of grace 1814, and the land around us was troubled much with war, a war in which neither The Builder nor I sought involvement yet which neither of us seemed able to avoid.

During the previous year the British and their Iroquois allies had killed more than nine hundred Americans in the Battle of Frenchtown and in the ensuing Raisin River Massacre. Then in August of that same year the Creek Indians too had apparently joined the British, attacking Fort Mimms in Mississippi Territory, killing over four hundred Americans and capturing five hundred more. In that atmosphere anyone with a red skin, or anyone found associating with someone who had one, was like as not to get shot. And therein lay the problem, the reason why both of us were being cautious. For I was white, and the person I was to meet was an Indian.

From where I stood hidden, on a hill that formed a point out into the water, several leagues of the valley of the Susquehanna lay before me. It was in the quiet of the early morning that I waited, a quiet so intense that a raven crying out on a ridge across the wide river sounded strangely out of place.

The mists of night were not yet dispersed, and thin tufts of moisture wafted through the tops of the trees below me, trees that for the most part were beech, maple, walnut, and oak. Around me the rhododendrons bloomed; the rhododendrons, the bluebells, and the dogwood, their perfumed blossoms making the air heavy with the sweet scent of spring. There was also the faint odor of smoke on the air, smoke from the breakfast fire of some farmer who was probably a descendant of one who had first settled the land, smoke which reminded me that the land around me was no longer wilderness, no longer wild and free.

Of a morning the beauty of the old Pennsylvania was still there, the beauty of a far and lonely country. But now, where silence had once reigned, and where Indians once had been the only inhabitants, with the beginning of day there would arise the constant sound of what some called civilization; the chopping of wood, the pounding of machinery, the explosions of gunfire, and above all else the incessant chattering of people. It was a thing that gave a man thought. Would the westward movement of whites never cease? I wondered. Would their craving for land never be satisfied?

Anxiously I rubbed my leg, waiting, hoping. The canoe, a dugout, was in sight again, briefly, as the Indian for whom I waited maneuvered skillfully around a large exposed boulder. But then, just as he disappeared once more into the darkness of the shadows, a musket shot rang out.

Instantly I was on my stomach, hoping that my homespun clothing would blend with the foliage. The shot had not been fired at me, I felt certain, yet I was not about to take any chances, not with so much at stake.

Cautiously I parted the ferns so that I could once again see down to the river. At first there was nothing, no sign of either the Indian or the one who had fired the shot. There was also no sound, nothing but the distant screeching of the raven. In fact, it was so quiet that I almost wondered if the musket shot had been my imagination.

Then I saw, floating out of the shadows, a long narrow log, and I knew that the shot had been real. The log had to be the dugout, now capsized. But where was the Indian? Where was the man I was to meet? Had they killed him? If so, where would that leave me?

"Sam," a voice floated up toward me, "I think you got him."

"I don't know," another voice responded. "I ain't so sure. Them redskins're tricky. But I reckon I did. He was here, just like the Huron said he'd be. And now maybe there's one more stinkin' British Indian out of the way. Where's his canoe, kid?"

"Down here, Sam, floating upside down. Say, Colonel, you want me to fetch it to shore?"

Another man responded positively, and then the voices became muffled and indistinct as the men gathered together.

With my heart pounding I carefully inched my way back into the thicket, wishing as I did that I was younger and had two good legs, for then my movements would not have been so painful.

Dead! The Indian, the man I longed to meet more than any other human being, was gone, killed by a patrol of what had to be the Pennsylvania Militia. Now what? I wondered. Was everything over? Had my dream, my escape and desperate ride, been for naught?

For a moment I thought back to my impressment, to the day the British had kidnapped me on the high seas and had pressed me into service on the British sloop *Frolic*. It was a common thing they had done, for many others had been kidnapped into British service. But such action was an evil thing, not to be tolerated, so impressment was one of the reasons the Americans gave, in 1812, for declaring war against the British.

For almost four years I had sailed aboard the *Frolic*, manning her eighteen guns and becoming, at least outwardly, a loyal British subject as well as an able-bodied seaman. For the first year I had thought of nothing but escape, but as the rumors of war began to fly, I determined to remain where I was. Though the *Frolic* was a small ship, her assignment was an important one, and much information came to her decks.

I had made it a point to obtain as much of this information as possible, for some day I might be able to use it in some way to stop the war. For while by birth I was an American citizen and sympathetic to my country's interests, by nature I was a man of peace, and by choice I had attempted most strenuously to dispel enmity between my fellowmen. Yet now, when my chance to make a significant contribution toward a peaceful settlement of the seemingly eternal conflict among men had finally arrived, it appeared to have been snatched just as quickly from my grasp.

The intensity of my desires for peace flashed before me and I wondered for the thousandth time why I felt as I did. It was certainly not customary for a man to feel so in an age when war and violence dominated the thoughts and hearts of most of the civilized world. A man's life meant little to others, and all too often it meant even less than that to himself.

Yet from my earliest memories I had respected life and had longed for a sense of brotherhood to flourish upon the earth. For years I had felt alone in that desire, and then only recently I had learned of another who seemed to share the same desires and goals as myself. He was the Indian I had hoped to meet; the one known as The Builder.

Additionally, there were the dreams. I was still not certain what to make of them, for all my life I had been of a practical nature, little given to placing much stock in less than tangible things. Yet now, in these past four years, I had dreamed three times, and none of the dreams would leave me. Each dream was different, and in each dream I had learned, or had seemed to learn, an entirely separate thing.

And that was a major part of why my meeting with the Indian had been so important. I felt that I had dreamed of him in one of my dreams, and I needed to know of the truthfulness of my dream.

Whap!

The smack of a rifle ball into a tree near me corresponded almost exactly with the explosion of a gun and harshly interrupted my reverie. Instantly I hunched even closer to the ground, wondering how I had been discovered. I had seen no one, had not shown myself, and had made no sound.

Without warning, a wet hand was suddenly across my mouth, the point of a knife was in my back, and I was being pulled downhill into the dogwood behind me. And though I am a large man and am rarely pushed about by others, my captor's movements with me seemed almost effortless.

For an instant I stiffened, preparing to offer resistance. But then I began to relax, sensing that I was in no danger. Almost immediately I was released, and rolling over I found myself looking up into a pair of dark and gentle eyes. Frantically my mind groped for understanding, for there, gazing down toward me, were the soft and oval eyes of a woman, an Indian woman who was dripping wet.

For an instant I stared in shocked silence, and the face above me seemed just as shaken. But the surprise on the Indian woman's face was only a flicker, nothing more, and my own expression lasted little longer.

As I opened my mouth to question what was happening, she motioned me to silence, whispered that the Huron was nearby, and signalled for me to rise and follow. Cautiously I obeyed, and I was soon trailing the incredibly silent form of this Indian woman, who was even then making her way with obvious ease through the dense brush away from the river.

For perhaps thirty or forty minutes we moved silently, neither of us speaking. With each step my mind searched for understanding, for ahead of me, dressed as a warrior, was an Indian *woman*. Initially my mind could conceive of her only as a guide, one who was to lead me to the man I was to meet. Gradually, however, as I followed her movements, doing my best with my bad leg to keep up with her, I became convinced that before me, moving swiftly and silently through the trees, was the one I had traveled so far to see, the one known as The Builder.

As my mind settled on her identity, I found myself wondering what manner of person she could be. Though she obviously was

smaller in stature than I, her agility and endurance were incredible.
I was also startled by her age. For some reason I had thought that
the Indian who was called The Builder would be younger, but the
woman's long and flowing hair was streaked with grey, and lines
of age were etched deeply into her face. She was at least as old as I,
and very likely even older. In short, she was a woman well into
her fifties.

But the thing about her that seemed most strange, the element
that surprised me most, was that in addition to her appearance,
even her ways seemed familiar to me. From the moment I laid eyes
upon her it was as though I had known her for as long as I could
remember. Perhaps it was because we somewhat resembled each
other, for we did in many ways. But then perhaps it was something else, too. As we walked I spent some time considering it,
trying to recall some memory of her at Donegal Springs. But none
would come, and I had to give up.

For more than a league we pressed forward in silence, and only
once in that time did we see the American militia. They were
riding down a ravine less than a quarter-mile away, searching back
and forth through the brush for the Indian they had lost at the
river, the Indian they now seemed to think had somehow survived. We hid, crouching in silence until their horses had passed
from sight, knowing as we waited that those men would yet need
to be dealt with.

Long moments after they had gone, the woman signalled me to
my feet and indicated a change of direction, and again we moved
forward, going even farther away from the river. At last, cresting
a hill, she silently cautioned me to wait. Then, almost eerily, she
vanished into the trees below.

A short time later she reappeared, and nodding with apparent
satisfaction, led me into a small and sheltered cove just below the
brow of the hill. It was a tiny area of not more than thirty feet in
breadth, and its surrounding rocks and trees made it a wonderfully secluded place. Once there, this remarkable Indian woman
sank to the ground before me. After a moment I did the same,
favoring my gout-filled leg as I did so. When, I wondered, would it
ever stop aching?

"It is well," she said softly and, surprisingly, in perfect English.
"We are alone, brother, at least for a time. I have laid a false trail,

and it will be several hours before the Americans can unravel it. The Huron alone causes me concern, but he dislikes the Americans so much that he will not help them. That would not be so, however, if he knew my identity. Then nothing would stop him. However, I feel certain that he does not know. Even from the Huron, brother, we should be safe."

Quickly then, and yet without hurry, she scooped together a small mound of twigs and leaves, struck a spark with flint and steel, and before long had a small fire flickering between us.

As I watched her movements I felt compelled to remain silent, sensing that it was not yet time for either of us to speak. The Builder, seemingly oblivious to my presence, removed from a red cloth pouch a highly decorated stone pipe. Filling the bowl with sacred tobacco, she lit it with a stick from the fire, inhaled deeply, and blew smoke to the four directions. Inhaling again, she blew smoke to the sky, and last of all toward the earth. Then, with solemn dignity, she passed the pipe to me.

I was surprised that she was performing what I had thought was essentially a man's ritual. Yet she seemed perfectly natural doing it, so I held my peace, followed her example, and smoked the pipe. Still she did not speak, and not wishing to offend, I too remained silent, waiting. Finally she began.

"So at last we meet, Malcom O'Connor. You have seen more winters than I had expected."

"As with you, Andaggy," I said, feeling the name roll awkwardly from my tongue.

"It is so," she said, smiling. "Always we see the seasons in others, but never in ourselves."

We both smiled then, and for the second time I felt a sense of trust and warmth in the presence of this woman, this Indian who was called The Builder.

"I have heard much of you, Andaggy," I said carefully.

"Yes," she replied, "I have been told that my name has been spoken freely by others. But Malcom O'Connor, I know little of you, save what the courier told me. I would know more of the reasons behind your own quest for peace. I would know why your desire to meet me was so great."

"Er ... well ... er ... ," I stammered, uncertain of how much I dared tell her. I could talk for hours of my feelings and desires, but that would be no answer. Yet would the woman mock if I told her of the dreams? Or was it appropriate that I speak of them at all? Of course, I could tell her about our common background.

"Brother," the woman said softly, interrupting my thoughts, "you seem hesitant. Yet it was you who pleaded that I come to this place."

"Yes, Andaggy, I did. And I would tell you all, save for—"

"Malcom O'Connor, the courier mentioned a dream. I would hear of that."

I was surprised, for I had spoken of my dream only in passing to the old friend who had found this woman for me.

"Well," I admitted hesitantly, "there was a dream . . . or dreams. Only, I don't know if they meant anything, and—"

"Brother," the Indian responded, sounding almost scornful, "I do not understand the thoughts of the white man. Among my people there is no medicine which has greater power than does a dream. Dreams give a person his name and set for him his pathway through life. Dreams are one of the methods used by the Creator to show his children his thoughts. Why is it that white men fear to admit or to accept such gifts?"

She continued, ignoring the surprise which must have shown on my face. "Brother, over the seasons of my life, though I am a woman, there have been enemies. As it stands, I know little enough of you. Perhaps you too are an enemy, as is the Huron who fired at me earlier, and who now searches for us near here. And perhaps this council which you have requested is a trap. I have given this thought careful consideration.

"Yet the courier spoke of a dream, Malcom O'Connor, a sacred vision of the night. Brother, a man does not speak lightly of his dreams, nor does he twist the truth concerning them. When I learned of your dream I thought I learned too of your heart, and thus I sent out a voice of agreement."

"I apologize, Ma'am," I said, feeling deeply embarrassed. "There was indeed a dream. In fact there were three of them. But they were confusing to me, and I had hoped that your words would help to clear my thoughts. If that should occur, then I will speak freely of them. Can you trust me enough to wait until then?"

For a moment the woman gazed silently into my eyes, and I suddenly realized that I was perspiring freely. Jumping ship had not made me anywhere near as nervous as did this woman's gaze. Yet I remained still, and at last she smiled and nodded.

"It is well," she said. "I will trust you, and will wait to hear of your dreams. I will also do what I can to give growth to your understanding. Yet it will be difficult, for how can I know what to tell you?"

"If you will permit it," I answered quickly, "I will ask you questions. Believe me, Andaggy, when I tell you that I sense something here which I do not understand, but which is so real that it frightens me. If your answers, whatever they may be, are given fully, I sense that the riddle of my life will be solved. Only then, Andaggy, when I know me, will I be able to truly help others as you now do."

"Very well, Malcom O'Connor. But remember that our time together is short. We have at most until the lying down of the sun. And should the militia find our trail, we will have even less time than that. You see, my people on the Ohio await me and the message I have been given for them. On this day, nothing is more important than their need. Speak, therefore, and we shall see what comes of this day."

The Riddle

"Thank you," I said sincerely. "First, Andaggy, I would know of your thoughts on peace, and of the reasons behind your search for it."

The Indian woman looked at me very carefully, took a deep breath, and began.

"Once, Malcom O'Connor, when I was younger, an old woman who was very wise gave me this riddle. She said:

A man has
a mare,
and the mare has
a colt.
Four seasons it takes for
the colt to be born,
and two or three times four seasons for
the colt to become
useful.
The same man,
in a war,

will hide his horse, or protect it,
lest he lose it
instantly
to the flash of an arrow or the
thrust of a lance,
and grieve greatly.
     A man has
a wife,
and the wife has
a son.
Three seasons it takes for
the son to be born,
and many *times three seasons for*
the son to become
a man.
     Yet the father,
who has spent the seasons of his life
teaching and training
the son,
will let pride blind his eye,
or vengeance, and
will declare war.
The son too goes to war,
for he must learn to be
a man.
But in battle the
father
loses his son instantly to
the flash of an arrow or the
thrust of a lance,
and his son is
no more.
Thus the father's grief is a
hollow thing,
for it is of
his own
making.
     Where,
I ask,

does the heart of
a man
lie?

"Brother," Andaggy continued, "the old woman's words gave me many long thoughts in later years, and when at last I understood their meaning, I set my heart for peace. Now I search for it with every breath I take. Without it, my people have suffered much, as have yours, Malcom O'Connor. And so, to help reduce that suffering, I have dedicated my life to the establishment of peace between them."

"Ah, and so have I, Andaggy, though truthfully I do not understand why. But tell me, why do you feel that peace between our peoples is so seldom found?"

"It is not an easy question that you ask, Malcom O'Connor. Yet I will do my best to answer you. However, the answer must be done with questions, questions which you must answer with your heart.

"Your country, brother, is now thirty-nine winters old. Before that, your people were here for perhaps as long as the lives of three old men. My people, those you call Indians, have lived here longer than the lives of many old men. Tell me, brother, to whom does this land belong?

"When your fathers came to these shores, my fathers welcomed them. We had much to teach, but even more to learn, and we gave thanks for that opportunity. But as the seasons passed, the Indians came to see that the white men did not understand the ways of true brotherhood. They were not willing to learn, or to give. Instead, they wanted only to take, to take, and to take. If anyone stood in the way of their taking, they were simply brushed aside like blades of grass in a strong wind. Always they were taking our lands from us, not sharing as we wished to do, but hoarding, taking always, without ceasing.

"Your people are now moving forward like a prairie fire, consuming everything that is in their path. Some of the red men are attempting to stamp out this consuming fire. But brother, I feel that it is too late. There are too many whites, their westward movement cannot be stopped, and many from both sides are suffering needlessly. I have thought long on this and feel only despair when I long for peace. How can it come? The ways of our peoples are so different, yet we have been thrown together suddenly. It has been as though neither of us has had the seasons to become used to the other, and it seems only natural that we fight.

"There is yet another thing which adds to this. Many among my people have adopted the taking ways of so many of the whites, and they no longer feel the old brotherhood. They are all the time filled with strong drink, trying to accumulate things so that they can purchase more strong drink, or else they are simply out creating trouble for the pure joy of being evil. They now think and act like many whites, with great selfishness, and the good spirit of the earth has departed from them. To get money or favors they sell still more of our land, a land which is not ours to sell, for it belongs to the Creator. And yet, a few red men, their greed encouraged by your people, sell this sacred land and cause many others to suffer needlessly. Brother, there is a great injustice here."

"You are right, Andaggy. There *has* been much injustice, but methinks if you knew the past of my people, of the white man, you would understand them better. For centuries, in Europe, the only ones who enjoyed the privileges of freedom were those few who had ownership of the land. The others, the majority, were considered less than equal. They were servants, and those who owned land looked upon them as serfs, mere chattels.

"But then this continent, your land, was discovered. To you it was home, well used, but to my people, who had always been oppressed and stifled because they could obtain no land, this country seemed a vast and unused wilderness of opportunity and freedom. Here was their chance, at last, to own land, to become free men.

"Can you blame them, Andaggy, for wanting to crawl from beneath oppression, for wanting to better their lives, for wanting to own and work their own land?"

"No, brother," the woman replied quietly, after a moment's thought, "I do not blame them. Nor do I blame those white men who have been born on these shores, for it is in their minds that it is their land as much as it is ours. And aren't they right? Is it wrong for them to want to claim it, and to use it? I cannot say that it is. As I see it, brother, the conflict is not between right and wrong, but between different views of what is right. And that causes me much sorrow. But Malcom O'Connor, even greater sorrow burdens my heart when I see that these differences cannot be resolved without bloodshed. Tell me, why is that?

"Two months past, when your General Andrew Jackson, known to my people as Sharp Knife, destroyed the Red-stick Creeks at the battle of Horseshoe Bend, he was only doing his best to protect the white frontier settlers. Or so he thought. But brother, the Creeks were also protecting their homes and families. Or so they thought. Tell me, brother, which of them was right? Were either of them? Or did they even have a choice in what they did?"

"There are no answers to those questions, Andaggy."

"Perhaps not, brother. Perhaps not. Again, think of this. The great Shawnee leader Tecumseh, who was killed last fall in the battle of the Thames River in Canada, and his one-eyed brother Tenskwatawa, who was known to us as the Prophet, did much to unite our people and to make them once more one with the earth. Was it wrong for Tecumseh to do what he did? Was it wrong for him and his brother to try to unite our people and to bring us again to the old ways? The answer, brother, is no.

"But, once united, my people turned against your people and tried to drive them from our ancestral homes. In doing so they caused much death and misery, which cannot be a good thing.

"The whites, doing their best to protect themselves, sent a General Harrison and his army against our people, and the Battle of Tippecanoe was fought. All of our homes at Prophetstown on the Tippecanoe River were burned, our food supplies were destroyed, and many of our people took the dark road of death to the west, including our women and children. Again, brother, who was right?"

"Andaggy," I said slowly, "there seems to be no answer, none at all. But it is easy for me to see why you have been called The Builder. With words you build pictures, pictures which show much insight. It takes great wisdom to see injustice on all sides of an issue, and the pictures you have built tell me that you do."

"Your words are kind, brother, but my heart is *not* kind! It tears at me constantly, and I get no rest. I am as a woman possessed, for I love my people and see that they have suffered much injustice. Yet so have the whites. Is there nothing that can cure this evil sickness called hatred? Is there nothing that will build a true brotherhood between our peoples?"

In the silence which followed Andaggy's anguished question we both gazed beyond each other, unseeing, each of us absorbed in his own thoughts.

Overhead the sun shone warmly upon us, and two squirrels chattered noisily in a beech tree nearby. It was such a tranquil scene that I found it difficult to recall that our land was buried in war and bloodshed.

I thought then of the four men who had led our country, our country which was and yet was not truly ours. Each of the four— Washington, Adams, Jefferson, and for the past five years Madison—were good men. As such, each had felt strongly the need to treat the natives of our land with fairness and equity. Yet none of them had been able to anticipate or to control the westward surge of American settlers, none of them could turn back the calendar to the point at which there were no whites in America, and none of them could conceive, nor convince others to conceive, that lands which seemed unused were not simply open for settlement. It was a vicious circle, with no apparent solution and no end that I could see. No end, that is, unless my dreams were valid.

For some time then the Indian woman and I sat together, each of us relating to the other what we knew of the war, of its causes, and of situations which might help to bring about its speedy conclusion.

I told her, among other things, of the three-pronged attack which I had learned was going to be launched by the British against the Americans within the next few months.

"The first prong," I said, "will be an army sweeping south out of Canada. The second prong will come up from New Orleans and push aside all opposition in the west. The third and final prong will sweep into the Chesapeake Bay, attempt to destroy Washington, and move inland from there. These three attacks, the British hope, will immobilize the United States and bring this land again under British rule."

"Brother," Andaggy said, "it is good to know this, for my people to the westward will once again be caught between whites. That is not a good place to be. However, there is yet hope.

"Three suns past I met with your General George Rogers Clark, who is known to my people as Big Knife. Though he walks now with only one leg, and though he is bitter, his words still carry great power, and he says much good concerning my people. With his brother, William, who helped lead the great expedition to the Pacific just eight winters past, a meeting has been called with the chiefs of all the western tribes. William Clark and General Harrison have been secretly authorized by some of the white leaders in Congress to promise my people all lands west of the Mississippi, forever, if we will no longer shed the blood of the whites. This news of the British attack on New Orleans will do much to influence the decisions of my people."

"Andaggy," I said softly, "the British promised you the land west of the Alleghenies back in 1763. The Americans promised you all of the lands west of the Ohio in the Greenville Treaty of 1795. Neither nation has kept its word. Can you now trust this new promise?"

"My brother," Andaggy said, sadly shaking her head, "I do not think so. Yet neither do my people have a choice. It is either this or more bloodshed for both of our nations.

"But now I have news which you must know. Simon Girty, the American renegade, is in Canada, where he lives his days in a drunken stupor. He will never again incite my people to war. As well, Matthew Elliot, the British Indian agent who has also done much to incite the Indians against the Americans, has recently taken the black road of death."

"Matthew Elliot? I have heard a great deal of that man. His name is notorious throughout the states. Though I do not like to say this, Andaggy, his death should help the cause of peace."

"Yes, brother, that is so. Though of course Matthew Elliot was a good and dedicated man too, in his own way."

"You know," I said, suddenly remembering something, "I once knew a Matthew Elliot. When I was but a lad living at the Donegal Springs, which is near where we now sit, a Matthew Elliot came frequently to visit. I wonder..."

For an instant the woman's face registered surprise, but then it was gone and I wondered if I had actually seen the expression. At length, though, she spoke.

"Brother, it is the same man. I know a little of him, and can tell you that he came from Donegal in Ireland to this place. With the great War of Independence he went toward the setting sun, first to the Scioto, then to the Great Miami. From there his path led to the Maumee, the Detroit, and finally to the lake called Ontario, where he took his black road, ever loyal to the cause of Great Britain.

"But enough of Matthew Elliot. Brother, you spoke of Donegal Springs, and of once having lived there. How is that so?"

"My family," I said, excited at her interest, but not ready to pursue it, "lived there until I was in my seventeenth year. We then removed ourselves to New York. Why do you ask?"

"It is a strange thing, brother. There is much that is the same between us, and now this too is the same. I also spent a few seasons near this place, near Donegal Springs, but was forced to leave when my people were destroyed. But brother, there is something more between us which I feel but do not yet understand."

For a moment I looked at the woman, aware that she was struggling intently with her emotions. When finally I spoke, the words came quietly, almost in a whisper.

"Andaggy, let us come back to that a little later, for I too feel it. For now, though, I would hear of your quest for peace and of the reasons behind it."

Slowly the woman lifted her head until she was gazing directly into my eyes. For long moments she sat thus, without moving, while I did my best to remain patient.

"Brother," she finally said, "this again is a strange thing. Why do I so strongly desire peace when the blood of my family has been so freely shed by others? Why has my heart not turned to stone with anger, revenge, and hatred? Ah, if only I could tell it all! But perhaps I can . . . a little.

"The answer, brother, is because of another woman . . . the old woman I spoke of earlier, the old woman with the riddle. She was a woman of many names. Yet the name which was most important, the one I would speak of, was the Peace Woman. Brother, the Peace Woman was my grandmother. I would tell you of the seasons of her life."

The Season of
New Green Growing

"The old woman who was my grandmother told me once that she did not truly live until the day she nearly died. Brother, I will speak of that, for on that day her own season of new life began.

"It was a season much as this one is now, and the hills were walking in the beauty of new green growing. Everywhere the wings of the air were making their songs of new life, the four-footeds too were dancing the mating dance, and it was truly a season of joy.

"For the people of my grandmother, the Susquehannocks, or People of the Falls, there was also much happiness. True, there were not many warriors left among them, for the dreaded white man's sickness, smallpox, had stalked through their village, sending fiery arrows everywhere. Yet for those who had lived to remember, the new season was a time of joy, and my grandmother's people were living it fully.

"My grandmother, whose name then was Kyunqueagoah, or the Flowers Which Grow Among The Stones, was in the woods with her sister gathering berries for the first fruits of the earth festival. It was a happy time, for the two sisters were taking much pleasure in each other's company. Let your heart be one with mine, brother, and we will be there together."

"Hiyii!" Stone Flower shouted shrilly. "Come, sister, look at these! Since our father the sun first kissed the leaves on the trees we have not seen such large and juicy berries."

Dropping to her knees, the young Indian maiden began filling her hickory-splint basket with the huge strawberries. She was a striking girl with long glossy black hair which fell to below her hips. On one side of her head a portion of her hair had been rubbed with bear fat and vermillion. This gave it added beauty, for as yet she had chosen no man in marriage. Her clothing consisted of quilled moccasins, short leggings that came up to her knees, and a wraparound skirt made of a rectangular piece of deerskin. The skirt closed over the right thigh so that when she knelt it fell open, thus exposing the calloused firmness of her leg. Then, whenever she had a free moment, she would twist bits of grass or bark on her exposed thigh, making cordage, thin rope that was used for shelters, fishtraps, and snares. Everything about her was beautiful and yet functional, for her people lived from day to day and could afford no wasted time or motion.

The men were the same, chipping stone points, making new weapons, and so on. For these People of the Falls there was no time to simply sit and do nothing. All needed to keep busy in order for each to survive.

The woman's sister, a little older, looked much the same except that her hair was braided and her forehead painted with vermillion, signifying that she was a new bride.

"Oh, sister," Stone Flower said excitedly, as she quickly filled her basket. "Never have I seen such berries as these!"

"Yes, they are large, but do not eat them," the older one cautioned.

"Oh, hush," giggled the one who kneeled. "Do you suppose that I would be so foolish? And yet, I must confess that I long to pluck such a berry as this one, and then fill my mouth with the sweet juiciness of it."

"Hah, silly girl," her sister said scornfully. "It should be that way with you and a husband. You should long to pluck one of them so that your womb would swell with the sweet fruits of marriage. You are long past the season when girls of the People become mothers."

"Ah, yes," Stone Flower replied wistfully, hanging her head with shame. "I suppose that you are right. But who is there to choose, I ask? I feel nothing for any of our warriors, and—"

"Look!" the older one suddenly said. "Our little sister the butterfly is waiting on your shoulder. She . . . now she is going! Look, my sister! She would lead us to ever larger berries. Come, this is a good sign. Let us follow."

Quickly the two women scrambled to their feet, and laughing excitedly they began following the butterfly more deeply into the thick forest. However, after a few moments the butterfly floated effortlessly up through the trees and out of sight, leaving the two sisters alone in a small clearing. As they paused, laughing and giggling and out of breath, the younger sister suddenly held up her hand.

"Shhh," she whispered, obviously puzzled. "The trees are filled with birds, and yet they are silent. The day is too young for these sisters to sleep. Something in this place has disturbed their work, and they warn us by their stillness."

"But I don't—" the older sister had started to say, when from behind her came a sudden shrill scream.

Spinning around, the two women were instantly knocked sprawling by the grotesquely painted forms of five Miami warriors. More surprised than afraid, Stone Flower and her sister leaped to their feet and, twisting away from their attackers, fled in different directions into the trees. That was to be the last that Stone Flower would ever see of her sister.

With a tremendous war-whoop three of the warriors came after her, and after perhaps a half-mile of desperate running they overtook her and threw her to the ground. Twisting around onto her back, Stone Flower found herself held firmly to the ground by a huge, well-proportioned warrior. Immediately sensing the futility of further struggle, she relaxed and was still, awaiting the right moment to again attempt an escape.

But there was no time, for instantly she was jerked to her feet, and her three attackers, ignoring the fear and agony which quickly filled her eyes, arrogantly pushed her forward as they began running single file through the trees. For a seemingly endless length of time they forced her to run in silence, first the two warriors, then herself, and last her huge and overpowering captor.

They had not gone many miles before Stone Flower's lungs were burning with an agony she had never before experienced. Her legs felt like leaden weights, and somewhere she had lost a moccasin, so that her foot was leaving bloody splotches on the ground where she ran. Only once she tried to break free, but the big warrior caught her easily, beat her with the back of his hand, threw her to the ground, and bound her wrists tightly behind her back. Then, lifting her roughly to her feet, he pushed her forward, and her horrible ordeal continued.

During the course of the day she fell repeatedly. But her captors, intent upon their destination, ignored her pain as they kicked her to her feet and shoved her ahead of them. She was given no opportunity to think, to feel, to wonder about the fate of her sister, or to consider anything else. There was nothing but run, run, run, one foot before the other foot, again and again, ignore the pain, pretend it wasn't there. Run, run, run! Forever.

At last, late in the afternoon, the four travelers came to a stream where they paused to drink. Stone Flower, almost delirious, fell face forward into the water. There she would have drowned had not the huge warrior grabbed her hair and pulled her free.

For a moment, while she lay retching and gasping for breath, Stone Flower's three captors held an animated conversation. Though she did not understand their language, she somehow knew that they were deciding to camp there for the night.

When finally the decision was made, the warriors dragged the young girl to the center of a small clearing. There the big man who was her captor stretched her arm out straight and bound it to a young tree. He then roughly took her other arm and legs and bound them to other trees in the same manner. For a moment then the three warriors simply stood, looking down at her and gloating over their success.

In fear Stone Flower turned her face away from them and closed her eyes. She had no idea of what to expect, for never had she been treated in such a way. Her people, the Susquehannocks, were a peaceful nation who greatly revered their women and

treated them with the utmost courtesy and respect. What, she
wondered, was wrong with these men that they did not do the
same? Had they been mistreated by their mothers, or what? Their
behavior was something which she simply could not comprehend.

As Andaggy spoke I could vividly imagine the scene as it must
have unfolded. Nor was it an unusual scene, for kidnapping and
slavery were common practices among many of the Indian tribes,
and my own people were guilty of the same atrocity as regarding
the Africans. Everyone, it seemed, used other people for their own
selfish ends.

"Andaggy," I said as she paused, "that was indeed a bad day
for your grandmother. But you have said that it was also a good
day. How is it that such a thing was so?"

"Brother," she continued in her soft, almost melodious voice,
"the good came about in this way. Stone Flower said that once she
was tied down, one of the warriors made a lewd gesture, and then
laughed at his idea. Instantly the other one, the large warrior who
had captured her, angrily pushed the smaller man aside. For long
seconds the two men glared at each other. Suddenly the smaller
one gave a war cry and lifted his tomahawk, whereupon Stone
Flower's huge captor shot him with his fuzee.

"In her telling then, my grandmother spoke of the two remaining warriors, who upon the death of their comrade commenced
immediately to argue over whose property she was. Ere long the
argument grew heated, and it was not many moments before it
was obvious to each of them, including my grandmother, that no
agreeable solution regarding her disposal was possible. At that
point the smaller Indian, who was apparently the leader, determined to conclude the matter without losing either his own life or
the life of his angry comrade. Without hesitation he raised his own
tomahawk and strode toward my grandmother, intending no
doubt to eliminate the basis for conflict which was staked out
between them."

Stone Flower watched with terrified fascination as the warrior
strode toward her, his ominous silence much more fearful than his
shrieking would have been. He was holding his tomahawk out
before him, and she realized suddenly that she was only seconds

away from death. For an instant she visualized her own scalp swinging from the man's breechclout next to the others he wore, and then she turned her head away in horror.

Shuddering with fear, she waited for the lethal blow to blot out her life. But as his shadow fell across her, there was a sudden explosion from a nearby thicket, and Stone Flower gasped in amazement as a crimson flower of blood blossomed upon her attacker's chest. As his already dead form fell across her body, she heard a loud war-whoop.

Twisting her neck, she was surprised to see a young white man leap through the cloud of gun smoke and into the clearing. He had dropped his gun and now carried only a long, gleaming knife which he held low in his right hand, the cutting edge turned upward. With great foolhardiness he advanced toward the remaining Indian, the giant who had first thrown her to the ground.

"Yeeeaaagh!" the warrior screamed, as he saw the white intruder. Then, sneering, he lifted his tomahawk, and grinning widely he threw it. There was a brief whirr as it spun through the air, and Stone Flower was sure the white man was dead. However, at the last possible second he jerked his head to the side so that the tomahawk flew harmlessly past and chunked heavily into a tree. As she saw the way the white man avoided the spinning weapon, Stone Flower felt the first faint glimmering of hope. Perhaps he was not a fool at all.

For an instant the giant warrior's grin vanished, but then he pulled out his own knife, leaped across Stone Flower's staked-out form, and cautiously advanced to confront his antagonist. Warily the two men circled, each silent, each intent on detecting and taking advantage of some weakness in the other.

For a moment they moved cautiously around the clearing, and then, suddenly, the white man dropped his shoulder, shifted his feet, and feinted a thrust with his knife. The warrior, fooled, stepped backward, and in the instant he was off balance the white man gave him a deep gash across his forearm. Startled, the Indian stared for an instant at his wound, scarcely able to believe that it was real. But then his grin reappeared, even wider, and confidently he inched forward, now stalking his prey.

The white man, not wanting to lose his advantage, stepped backward once, and then again. As he took his third step backward, however, a stick rolled beneath his foot, and momentarily he too lost his balance. The Miami warrior was instantly onto him, and with a scream of triumph he thrust forward and downward with his knife.

With swiftness born of desperation the white man twisted to one side, felt the knife slice across his ribs, and then kicked, catching the Indian squarely on the knee. Grimacing, the warrior staggered backward, the white man rolled over and scrambled to his feet, and both stood breathing heavily and staring into each other's eyes.

Suddenly the warrior lunged forward, and with a howl of rage he swept his opponent's knife aside, picked the white man bodily off the ground, and threw him into a clump of dogwood. Sensing victory then, he hurled himself on top of the smaller man. Grabbing the white man's hair and twisting it in his fist, he brought his knife forward to remove the scalp.

The young white man, still groggy from his fall, saw the flash of the knife an instant too late. Unable to twist away from the descending weapon, he threw his forearm upward and blanched as the blade slammed through the flesh and into the bone of his arm.

Doing his best to ignore the pain, he utilized the momentum of the warrior's swing, heaved upward with his body, and threw the Indian over his head and onto the ground. Spinning then, the two men pulled themselves to their feet and stood apart, their lungs raking in great heaving gulps of air and their legs shaking with pain and exhaustion.

Both men were covered with sweat, blood, and dirt, and Stone Flower, transfixed by the horror of the scene before her, felt certain that the battle was nearly over. In the early evening stillness a fly buzzed past, and the Susquehannock maiden wondered that her tiny sister the insect was so anxious to begin her work upon the dead.

Without warning the warrior feinted, and then with a rush he closed in on the white man. His knife was held low, and the look on his face showed clearly the hatred he felt for his enemy. For an instant the two men scuffled together, straining against each other with every fiber of their bodies.

Suddenly the white man gave a gasp and thrust upwards. The warrior slowly rose up to his full height, towering several inches above his white antagonist. With careful precision he raised his knife above him into the air, and in an instant the air was shattered with his piercing, strident scream. Then, as both Stone Flower and the white man watched in silence, the warrior's fingers loosened, his knife slid slowly from his grasp, and his huge frame collapsed loosely to the ground.

For a short while the white man put his hands on his knees, and with his head hanging he sucked in huge gulps of air. Finally, after wiping his crimsoned blade on a clump of grass, he turned and, staggering a little, made his way to where Stone Flower was bound.

Speaking gently, in a language which the Indian woman did not understand, the man took his knife and severed the thongs which held her rigidly between the trees. Carefully then he extended his open hand and helped her to her feet.

Sensing that the frightened woman was about to flee, the man took hold of her wrist and began sawing at the thongs which still encircled it. Suddenly, however, he began to sway back and forth, almost as though he were drunk. Realizing that he was about to lose consciousness, he quickly placed his knife into the hands of the girl, turned, and fell unconscious to the ground.

For an instant Stone Flower backed away, irresolute. But she quickly made up her mind, hurried to the fallen man, rolled him over, and found blood seeping not only from his arm but from his side as well. Quickly, in the diminishing light of early evening, she began scurrying about, gathering herbs and bark. Then, with two pieces of dried wood and a section of the leather thong which had bound her, she improvised a bow and drill and soon had a small fire burning. In a hastily made bark container she heated water from the nearby stream, and with that she cleansed the man's wounds. Next she placed a compress of leaves and moss upon them, and finally she secured the compress with leather cut from the clothing of one of the dead Indians.

Later, in the almost total darkness, she dragged the bodies of her former captors away from the clearing, located the white man's packs, and set about constructing an efficient camp.

Throughout the long night Stone Flower attended the delirious white trader, for such he proved to be. In the morning, when he finally regained consciousness, the man made signs to her that he was an Englishman and that he had spent several years trading for furs with the various tribes. When Stone Flower signalled that she was Susquehannock, the man beamed, and immediately began speaking, though somewhat haltingly, in her own tongue.

"Thank you for saving my life," he said feebly. "My name is Roger Winslow. How are you called?"

"Kyunqueagoah," she answered shyly, suddenly confused by the man's forward and direct question.

"Ky . . . Kyun. . . . Ah, I'm afraid my tongue cannot make your name. I'll tell you what. While we are together, I'll call you . . . ah . . . let's see. Milly! That's a good name. Can you say that? Milly?"

"Meeleee," Stone Flower replied bashfully.

"Close," Winslow said, grinning. "Try it again. Milly."

"Mil-lee."

"Good! You are Milly. I am Roger. Can you say that? Roger?"

"Rogg . . . Rogg. . . ."

"That's right, Milly. That's right! Try it again. *Roger.*"

"No," Stone Flower said, her voice suddenly stern. "My tongue cannot make your name, as yours cannot make mine. But you are a hairy man, hair all over your face, not like the men of my people. I will call you Hairy Man. Can you say that? Hairy Man?"

"But . . . but . . ." Winslow stuttered, "it's just my beard, and—"

"Say it!" Stone Flower encouraged chidingly. "Say 'Hairy Man.' "

For a moment Winslow looked closely at the young woman, nearly offended. But then he saw the twinkle in her eye and realized that she was simply stating her equality. He laughed and, stroking his beard, held out his hand.

"Fair enough," he said. "Here, Milly. Let us shake on it. You and Hairy Man have an agreement."

"You see, brother," Andaggy said softly, "though my grandmother's life nearly ended that day, it also began. It was both a bad day and a good day."

I nodded quietly, for I could indeed "see." The woman had an incredible ability with words, and she seemed able to make past events come alive. Yet for me it was still not enough. What I was hearing was what I had come so far to hear, of that I was certain.

Yet it was still not enough. I had to keep the Indian woman talking. Somehow I had to encourage her so that I could hear all of her story of the Peace Woman.

In the short silence which followed her last statement I noticed a flock of chickadees fluttering around a large sugar maple tree a little below us on the slope. The woman also took notice, or she saw that I did, for she suddenly spoke of them.

"My brother," she said, "in that tree yonder is the wigwam of my little sister the chickadee. She is least in strength but strongest of mind among her kind. She is willing to work for her wisdom, for she is a good listener. Nothing escapes her ears, and yet in all her listening she tends to her own business.

"My grandmother was like the chickadee. She was a good listener, and she wished always to learn new things. By the time she and Roger Winslow arrived back at the Susquehannock village on Conestoga Creek, a journey of several days, she had already learned much of the white man's language and of his ways. She had also learned that her heart wanted this man for her husband.

"Among our people, brother, women were much honored, and had great power and authority. They were givers-of-life, along with the Great One above, and were revered as much as he and our true mother, who is the Earth, were revered. In our tribe, brother, the women were as important as the men. They were the real rulers in the village as the men were the rulers in the chase and in war. Even in these latter things the women often advised the men and restrained them from being overzealous and hasty, and then men listened to them. The women owned property and retained that property in marriage. They had their own societies and guilds. A woman who could make a fine lodge was as important as a man who was a good hunter. No woman was given in marriage without her consent. Strong persuasions may have been spoken by her parents or by the brother or uncle who may have owned her in the sense that he was in charge of her disposal in marriage, but she was never forced. Her person was respected by all men at all times and in all places as long as she herself respected it. She was not a drudge, a chattel, a slave. She was a Susquehannock woman.

"Each of our clans, brother, consisting of blood relatives through the mother's side of the family, was controlled by an elderly woman. She would not necessarily be the oldest woman, but she was chosen because of her wisdom and the respect which others gave to her.

"In the clan controlled by this woman we were all one family, much closer than you white men can think or understand. The son of my aunt was my son; the daughter of my aunt was my daughter. My brother's son was my nephew, the son of my nephew was my grandson. My brother's daughter was my niece, her son was my son, and the daughter of my niece was my daughter. Also, the children of this son and daughter were my grandchildren. In such a way, brother, one was never without close kin in times of trouble.

"Our people had a council of these beloved women, and this council did much in the way of leading our people. They approved marriages, and they coordinated the economic activities of the female clan members—not only their work in the fields, but also their giving of food for charity and public festivals.

"When one of the sachems or chiefs died, my brother, it was up to the matron of his lineage, in consultation with her female relatives, to select his successor. If the new leader's conduct was not satisfactory, the matron would warn him three times, giving him a chance to improve. After that the matron would ask the council to depose him. Because of her position it was necessary for the matron to always conduct herself with great decorum so that when she had to admonish an erring chief her words of warning were heeded.

"To the beloved woman, the matron of the turtle clan, came my grandmother, Stone Flower, who was now so very anxious to be called Milly."

"Grandmother," Milly said, after waiting through an appropriate period of silence, "I have brought a man to our village, a man who is white and hairy of face, and yet a man who knows our people and understands their ways. He has taken the name of Hairy Man. Grandmother, though he has little to offer in trade, it is my desire to become his woman."

The old matron, very wrinkled and yet with surprisingly dark hair, nodded and smiled an almost toothless grin.

"Is this a heart decision, my daughter?" she asked. "Or is it a decision born of your mind?"

Milly sighed deeply. "This I do not know, Grandmother. He is different from us, and there is much that I would learn from him. That desire is indeed born of my mind. Yet when I am with him, Grandmother, something else stirs within me, and I feel a great warmth here in my chest. I long to touch him, and I tremble when I think about doing so. Is this a heart thing?"

The old woman nodded, smiling. "It is, my daughter, and it is a *good* thing. Do you know yet of this man's heart?"

"No, Grandmother, I do not. But we were alone together and shared our thoughts many times during our journey here. I feel that he is a good man. In addition, he risked his life for mine."

"These are good things. Bring the young man to me, my daughter. I will speak with him, and we will conclude this matter."

Springing to her feet, Milly excitedly ran to the small wigwam where Roger Winslow was resting.

"Come, Hairy Man," she said, pulling at his hand. "The old woman of the turtle clan wishes to speak with you."

Innocently unaware of what was taking place, Winslow arose from his bed of furs and followed the young woman through the village and into the bark longhouse where the old matriarch waited.

"Hairy Man," the old woman said in her high, squeaky voice, "Kyunqueagoah tells me that you understand our tongue. Yet you have never visited this village. How can this be so?"

"I have traded with others of your people, Grandmother. The Leaning Tree band, of whom you have no doubt heard, takes many furs for my people, the English. I learned what I know of your ways from them."

"Ah, that is good. Then you know, my son, that our people honor greatly the wishes of our women, for they are the givers-of-life to our nation."

"This I know," Winslow replied, uncertain about why the old woman was speaking of such things. The Indian girl whom he called Milly was standing behind the old woman, smiling, and the longer he stood in the smoky darkness of the longhouse the more uncomfortable he became. Something was going on, and he knew it. The trouble was, he did not know what, and it was to his lifelong good that he didn't.

"Ah, good!" the old woman continued. "Then you must also know, my son, that our women choose their men with their hearts. Once they make such a choice, it becomes my duty to join them together. Hairy Man, you have opened the heart of Kyunqueagoah, and she has chosen you as her man. We welcome you as one of our people. Now go, speak with her beneath the blanket. For our people, it will be as though you are alone on a mountaintop surrounded by a world of clouds."

"But . . . but . . . !" Winslow stammered.

"My son," the old woman said kindly, "may many children grace your wigwam. Now close your mouth, take your woman, and go. I am tired, and an old woman such as me needs much peace and rest."

Stunned, and yet sensing the futility of further words, Winslow slowly turned, took Milly's hand, and departed.

"And that was that?" I asked, a little surprised. "He and your grandmother were married?"

"Aye, brother," Andaggy replied. "The white man and my grandmother, from that moment forward, were husband and wife."

"Well, did it work? I mean, were they happy? Did they live at the Conestoga Creek village? Did they have any children?"

"So many questions, brother. Often I have been anxious to learn at the feet of the white man, and frequently I have been forced to so learn. But never have I had a white man who was so anxious to learn from me. You will forgive my surprise?"

When I grinned and nodded, Andaggy continued her story.

The First
Glimmerings

It was late autumn. The sun spent its time farther toward the south than before, went to bed earlier, and hid more often from the winds which howled menacingly in from the north. Yet in the wigwam of Hairy Man and Milly there was more than enough of warmth, of joy. And so it was that they almost failed to notice the coming of old man winter.

"Milly," Hairy Man asked one night as the cold wind whistled through the trees above their lodge, "are you happy?"

Aye, my hairy warrior, she replied softly.
The wigwam is tight,
my belly is full,
the furs beneath me are soft,
and your warmth beside me
is more than pleasant.
I am happy.

"And you would want nothing more?"

My husband, Milly responded quickly,

What more would I need to
be happy?
I am not as some of the women
of your people
whom I have met,
ever seeking but
never finding.
I am a
woman of the
Susquehannocks.
I am married to a
good man,
one who has
made me
comfortable.
I also have made him
comfortable.
I am content.
    But you, my husband,
are the one who
spoke of
happiness.
Are you not happy
with me?

    "With you," Hairy Man laughed, "I am more than happy. No man could ask for more."

    But do you not
miss your
people? Milly questioned.

    For a long time her husband lay quiet, thinking. At last he rolled over, pulled her close, and spoke.

    "Occasionally," he said, "I long to speak with the men of my people. I would speak with them of science, for I have learned much of the ways of the earth and wish to know more. I would also discuss with them religion, for you have helped me feel and understand things which, if shared, would likely help others as they have helped me with my beliefs."

    And the women? Milly asked gently.

Do you not wish
to speak with
them?

"Milly," he responded, "you are my woman. I speak with you, and it is as though I have spoken with all others. Beyond you I have no needs or desires. Beyond you there are no other women."

Ah, Milly smiled as she cuddled even closer,
your words fill my
heart with
happiness.
It is good that you and I are of
one people.

Together in silence they lay then, secure in the warmth of their love. Outside the winds of night drifted down from the hills and rattled against the bark lodge, sending exploring fingers under the edge and through the cracks in the side. In the trees above the limbs swayed back and forth, shivering in their new-felt nakedness, sending the sounds of their creaking into the wigwam below.

"Milly," her husband whispered. "Listen. The little people are talking. Out in the trees."

But my husband,
I hear only
the wind.

"Listen, Milly," Hairy Man urged, half jokingly. "Can't you hear them? They are speaking to us."

I am listening.
And still I hear only the
wind.
But if you hear them,
my Hairy Man,
what are they
saying?

"They say: Hairy Man, it is good that you are here in this place with your woman, with your people."

Milly laughed quietly, and as the wind continued to whistle through the trees she pressed even closer to her husband and spoke again.

I am happy that you have

learned of the
little people,
for they are our
friends.
Tell me,
what are they saying
now?

"They say: Hairy Man, this woman who is your woman is the best of all peoples. She is lovely as the light that creeps over the edge of the world when it chases after the star of the dawn. She is warm as the summer sun in the season of green growing things. She is comforting as the good sleep that comes in the night after a hard hunt. She is the best of all people for you."

Ha, Milly giggled.
They would not say that.
It is foolish
talk....
But it is good *talk, too.*
Tell me more of what
you say
they say....

"For that time, Malcom O'Connor, each brought much happiness into the heart of the other. They lived simply, as my people have done for more seasons than one can count. In a clearing near their wigwam they raised, during each season of growth, what my people called the three sisters—corn, beans, and squash. Hairy Man also picked the wild plums, and Milly stoned and dried them for the winter. He gathered quantities of the plentiful wild berries and she pounded them fine on a hollowed stone and made them into flat cakes and dried these for the cold weather. He gathered nuts, which were very many, and the wild grapes, which were few, and she prepared them too. These and other things helped fill the storehouse, which already held much meat from his hunts. She worked on the hides, which was woman's work and which she would not let him do, even though he traded for them always.

"While Hairy Man was away, either hunting or trading, Milly spent her time performing other woman tasks. She wove bark and grass containers to be used for storage, she manufactured fish traps out of cordage which she seemed always to be twisting against her thigh, she constructed a small wigwam designed only for travel so that she and the children which would come could accompany Hairy Man on his trading sorties, and she made all the clothing for the family, leggings, mantles, and moccasins. She beaded them as well, with beautiful designs of her own making. She also learned, with amazing speed, to speak his language. Do you see, brother, how this woman was like the busy chickadee?"

"Aye, Andaggy, that I do."

"Many times," she continued, "my grandmother spoke of the first time she accompanied her husband on a trading journey. She spoke of the endless hours riding a mule through the forest, of her surprise at how far the world stretched out in all directions, of the strange customs of the Indian peoples they encountered, and of the even stranger ways of the whites who lived in wondrously big villages to the east. The journey was a hard time for her, for the winds were cold and the snows were piled deeply in the valleys. Yet it was also a happy time, for she was with Hairy Man; again she was learning, satisfying her never-ending hunger for knowledge and understanding; and within her, new life was growing.

"On the day when Milly told her husband of the certain coming of their little one, she stood straight and proud. Within her she was doing what a woman alone could do, and what she was doing was very good. The glow of new life was upon her, and in all things she felt superior to the man who stood anxiously before her, the man who would never know the joy of giving life."

It will come, Milly said to Hairy Man, smiling,
*when the winter snows have
melted and the
trees begin to
bud.
Then, my husband,
will we truly be
one people.
Then will your son begin to grow
tall.*

Then will he learn to
love this earth as
we do.
Now truly am I
happy.

"Yet even while my grandmother and Hairy Man lived in happiness with their family, which soon became two sons, the whites were marching westward, creeping into our land just as the snow creeps into even the warmest lodge. My grandmother had watched William Penn sign his treaty with our people, and by the time she became the woman of Hairy Man, our valleys here along the Susquehanna were already filling with white farmers.

"These people, whites from beyond the sunrise sea, were not bad people. It was only that most of them somehow forgot, in their quest for new opportunity, that my grandmother's people were people at all. As the fingers of the white man grasped ever more frequently toward the lands of our ancestors, some among my people buried their ways of peace and began to fight back. It was after one such conflict that the season of my grandmother's life changed abruptly. It was then that she lost the silent ways of the chickadee."

"Milly," Hairy Man said quietly, speaking into the darkness, "we cannot become involved. We are in this Mohawk village as guests, and if we attempt to do anything, then our lives and the lives of our children will be of no value whatever."

And what of that? Milly asked in a rare burst of anger.
Must you think always
in terms of
value?
Do you never think
in terms of
right?

For a long time there was silence, and the two adults could hear plainly the distant chants of the Mohawk warriors.

My husband, Milly said finally,
I know that what you say is true,
and I honor your
thoughts.

But there is a bad feeling among
this people,
and as a woman of the
Susquehannocks
I cannot turn my head
from it.
    "But Milly, I—"
    Hush, my sweet and brave
Hairy Man.
It is best that you remain here,
in our lodge,
for there is much hatred against whites
in this place.
Even though you have traded with them often,
they are full of
French rum,
their eyes do not see clearly,
and you are in
danger.
    However,
I am kin to these people,
my husband,
for many of them are of the
turtle clan,
as am I.
Remain here while I go and
exercise
my right as a
woman.
I will be gone only so long
as it takes me
to nurse our youngest
child.

    Rising then, Milly adjusted her mantle about her shoulders, picked up her youngest son, and stepped out into the darkness.

    As her eyes adjusted, she could see a fire blazing brightly through the distant trees. Picking her way carefully across the snow, she worked her way through the forest until she stood at the edge of a large clearing.

In the open area Milly saw a group of perhaps fifty Mohawk women lined up in a double line, with a narrow aisle between them. All of them were shrieking with excitement, and as Milly watched she saw three white people, a woman and two young children, running naked between the women. As they ran, the Indian women on both sides whipped and beat them mercilessly, doing their best to stop their progress. Milly had never seen the gauntlet, but she had heard it described and she wondered that women and children were being put through it. Usually, she knew, it was used only to test men, and never those who were less strong.

Finally, near the end of the gauntlet, the woman fell to the ground. The children, hesitating, were also beaten to their knees, and as they groveled in the snow the shrieks of the Mohawks reached a fever pitch. Milly, watching, felt her heart sink, for she knew the significance of their failure.

Suddenly several warriors leaped into the melee and, dispersing the women, yanked the captives to their feet. Then they took them, bloody, bruised and still naked, and bound them to three upright posts which had been planted in the ground. The white woman, Milly could see, was oblivious to her own agony, but she was writhing in horror as she watched what was happening to her children. Those, terrified and in pain, were screaming and sobbing, but their pleas brought forth no mercy. They had failed the gauntlet, so they obviously did not have the courage to become Mohawks. They were cowards and deserved only to die. They could never be adopted.

As the Mohawks began piling faggots of wood around the prisoners so that they could be burned, Milly began to relive her own horrifying kidnapping of a few summers before. The terror was there—the terror and the horror she had felt when the Miami warrior had approached her with his upraised tomahawk. As Milly's mind returned to the present, she realized that her body was bathed in clammy sweat, and she knew that she had to stop what was happening. Somehow she had to save the lives of the captives—regardless of the color of their skin, regardless of their weakness under pain.

As the flames began to leap up around the three writhing forms, Milly darted into the circle of Mohawks, held her baby above her head, and kicked frantically at the flaming brands, scattering them way from the captives.

Instantly silence reigned in the circle, silence broken only by the now subdued sobbing of the white children. Ignoring the angry stares of the Indians, Milly finished scattering the flames and then with her knife she cut the three whites loose. After giving her mantle to the shaking white woman, Milly faced the Mohawks and slowly began to speak, her words coming quietly but firmly.

Ho, brothers.
A sister,
an honored woman of the
turtle clan,
a giver-of-life whose child you
see here before you,
takes hold of her right as
a woman
and lays claim to the
lives of these
people.
Here now my words.

Andaggy laughed lightly, apparently enjoying this particular memory. "I do not know," she continued, "all of the words my grandmother spoke to the Mohawks that night. I know a few of them and will speak them if you wish, for they carry much power and much goodness. They also point out the direction her life took from that night forward. Do you wish to hear?"

I nodded eagerly, anxious to hear the words of this strange woman who had been so long dead but whose life seemed so important to me.

Closing her eyes, Andaggy lifted her chin, squared her shoulders, and for the next few moments she became her grandmother, facing the Mohawks as she taught them the way of peace.

Brothers, she said clearly as she faced the stern visages of the Mohawk warriors,
I am a woman,
  I am a giver of life.

I am a woman,
    I hold up half of the sky.
I am a woman,
    I nourish half of the earth.
I am a woman,
    all things of beauty touch
    my shoulders and
    live before my
    eyes.
I am a woman,
    and stand as half of all things living.
I am a woman,
    and give life to all things.
    Brothers,
the father is the pale one,
and the grandfather is the Creator.
But the mother of us all is
the Earth,
she who gives us all we need
and yet who is humble enough to allow us to
walk upon her.
    This child that I hold
is of my own breath and
body, for I too am a
mother of life.
There is another son of mine,
not here,
who is of my breath and body
as well.
They are two,
yet they are one, for each of them is
of me.
    Should there be cruelty or hatred
between them,
I would send out a voice of
despair, of agony,
for my heart and my love would be
torn apart.

Does not our mother
the Earth
feel the same?
     We,
the four-leggeds, the trees, the wings,
and all two-leggeds,
are one also, for we are
children of our mother
the Earth.
We share the same breath,
and we walk the same paths through life.
Should we not walk as
brothers,
as sisters?
Should we not walk in beauty?
     Brothers,
great warriors do not always
fight,
but with wisdom are
the peacemakers,
the protectors of the
weak.
They are bearers of the
gentle heart.
I would show you the way.
     As an honored woman of the
People of the Falls,
and as a guest in your
village,
I exercise my right of decision and
take these three,
who are weak,
to my lodge.
When the sun rises again
they must be returned to
their own people.
     Think long thoughts this night,
my brothers,

concerning the old way, the way of
peace,
the way given us by the
Pale One,
for it is the way of
all true men.
   For this night, I have
spoken.

"Did she get away with it?" I asked incredulously. "Did the Mohawks let her get away with it?"

Andaggy nodded silently.

"Who were they? The captives, I mean?"

"This thing I do not know, brother. I know only that with first light the captives were returned, with gifts, to the place of their home."

"So that was the start of her peace mission," I concluded. "That was why she was called the Peace Woman?"

"No, brother," Andaggy replied softly. "Her name did not come until much later. But that indeed was the beginning, for in the darkness of that night sat another, a stranger to the camp of the Mohawks. When the sun went down again he sought out my grandmother, and it was his word which started her down the long and lonely road of peace."

"One last question, Andaggy. Who was the Pale One she spoke of?"

The woman looked at me for a moment and smiled.

"Brother," she said softly, "that is my next telling. Hear now my words."

The Legend

"Malcom O'Connor, the season which you call summer is what my people call the season of green growing corn. It is the season for young things to mature, so that they will become useful to other living things. I would tell you now of my grandmother's season of growing.

"She and Hairy Man and their two sons were one day away from the lodges of the Mohawks when the stranger made his presence known to them. My grandmother was roasting venison over a small fire and her sons were playing quietly nearby when the man suddenly appeared out of the darkness."

"Heyo," a man's voice called out from a little distance, "I would share your fire this night."

Startled, Milly looked out into the darkness and then glanced quickly around for Hairy Man. Yet he was not in sight, and for an instant she felt fear. However, when the man appeared his face was open and kind, and as she gazed upon him she sensed that he would do none of them any harm.

You are welcome here, Milly said pleasantly.
My sons and I honor
your presence,
and the white warrior who is my
husband
will do likewise upon
his return.
There is more than enough here,
of corn and of venison,
and you are welcome to
share with us.

Silently the man, who was tall and stately, made his way to the fire. There, with practiced ease, he lowered himself onto a bear-skin robe, taking her husband's place of honor. Surprised, Milly was about to object, but then, thinking better of it, she continued her preparation of the meal in silence.

In a short time Hairy Man returned, and he too was surprised to see the stranger who was seated in his place. With true polite-ness, however, he said nothing, but took another position across from the stranger, where he too waited in silence.

After an appropriate time he removed his pipe from its pouch, lighted it, smoked it to the four directions, and then passed it to the stranger. The tall man took it, repeated the ritual, handed it back, and then the two continued in silence, waiting for Milly to indicate that they should begin their meal.

Later, when all had eaten, the tall stranger took from his own pack a very ornate pipe, smoked it, passed it to Hairy Man, accepted it back after Hairy Man had smoked it, and put it away. Only then did he finally speak.

"It is good that we pay honor to the four directions," he said, "for this night I would speak of the one who taught us of their power. I am known as High Tree. I am a chief of the Seneca nation, which is part of the great confederacy. One sun past I sat in the village of my Mohawk brothers and watched as your woman freed three white captives. She then talked of peace and of the Pale One, and when she had finished, my heart spoke to me and told me that I must follow you here. Thus I have come."

"Our Seneca brother is welcome to our humble encampment,"

Hairy Man said gravely. "You may remain with us until your heart tells you to go elsewhere."

"Brother, your words are good, and this man hears them with much gratitude."

During the conversation between the two men, Milly had been feeling a strange sensation, yet she did not know how to respond. It was as though she had known this man before and had heard his thoughts. Before each thing was said she somehow knew what his words would be, and it unnerved her. For instance, she knew that he would next ask to speak with her as though no one else was near. The feeling was frightening, yet somehow she sensed that it was meant to be.

"Brother," the Seneca said, continuing, "it is within my heart to speak with the woman. Giver-of-life has much for her to do, and I would speak with her of it. I would know her name."

"I call her Milly," Hairy Man answered, "but her Susquehannock name is Kyunqueagoah. You are at liberty to speak directly with her."

Hairy Man settled back then, and with his two small sons on his lap listened intently as the tall chieftain spoke to his wife.

"Daughter," the man said gently, "hear with your heart the words I would speak. I call you daughter because this night I would be your teacher, your father. Your name signifies flowers among the stones, and that is good, for you truly shall blossom forth in hard and difficult places.

"Your words to the Mohawks were as a shaft of light to my heart, and it is within me to teach you more of the religion of peace, a religion which you know and yet of which you know nothing."

My father, Milly replied, feeling frightened and yet curiously eager to hear the man's message,
*tonight you are indeed
my father.
I truly know nothing of a
religion of
peace.
Yet my heart is strong,
and burns with the fire*

of hope
that all men might live
in harmony.
I await your words.

In the silence which followed, the Seneca chieftain reached out and added fuel to the fire. As the flames lifted brightly into the cold night air, the man sent out his words and began his telling. His voice was deep, and he spoke with a quiet dignity, speaking as though he had actually seen what he began telling Milly of.

"My daughter," he said, "I will tell you of a legend. Hear me closely, for it is perhaps the greatest legend among our people. Back beyond the lives of many old men there came among our people a bearded stranger. He was pale of feature, and his eyes were as gray-green as still water and just as changeable in their color. He was the Pale One of whom you spoke.

"No one knew the land from where he came, and yet he appeared with the star of the dawning, coming to us from out of the east. Thus he came to be known, among other things, as the Dawn God. As he came, the light from the early morning sun touched his hair with a sheen of red-gold, lighting it until it burned like newly mined copper. Without doubt he was a white man, and yet he was not as the white men we have come to know in recent times. This one was a god, and he came to us with high soul-stature, more even than I can say.

"Many things about this man were different, and at first our fathers feared him. He spoke our language without difficulty, and with no effort he saw into our hearts and knew fully of our ways. He wore a robe of white which descended to his feet, almost hiding his golden sandals. Around the bottom of his robe were sewn many crosses, which was the same sign that had been engraven upon his hands.

"When he stood before us, he raised his hand in greeting. As he did, one among the people, noticing the strange markings in his hands, asked him how he came by them. He would say no more than that he had been hurt in the lodges of his friends."

My father, Milly interrupted, questioning intently,
is this pale god the same
who is known to our people as
the Healer?

"Yes, daughter," the tall Seneca responded, nodding. "He is the same. It is said that when he touched a man who was wounded, that one became healed. Even the touch of his eyes gave comfort."

I have heard of this
ancient god,
my father,
from my own people.
But the memory is dim,
and I recall little
of him.

"Legends of this wondrous being are common," the Seneca replied, "though they are fast disappearing from among our people. It is said that he passed among all of our nations, telling them to be good, to do good, to *love* good. He walked and walked, always telling, and his appearance was more than lovely. His eyes were soft and seeing, so much so that he saw through men, and saw, and saw, and saw. Men and women, looking on, felt his love for them and wept. Then they stopped their wars and their hating, and so it was that their bows and arrows shot the deer, but never man again. Long our people walked in the way of the pale god, teaching their children of him. But then one great chief, a builder of big houses of stone, began to war again, and soon all of our people, save a few only, had lost the way of love."

But who was this man? Milly asked, feeling almost breathless with her excitement.
How was this
pale god
called?

"His names were many, my daughter. But sadly, I am not able to tell you more of who he was. It is said that he told the old ones his true name, but if he did, it has long been lost. Among the fathers of my own people he was known as Hea-wah-sah. This name means He-From-Afar-Off. Our neighbors to the north, the Chippewa, called him Wis-ah-co. He was also known by other names, but they were not so important as his message.

"When the white god came to our fathers, he brought them his religion, changed the temples, and taught them a sacred language with certain signs of greeting. These signs I do not know. But more importantly, my daughter, he taught all of our people his peace religion and told them that the mark, the cross engraven in his hands, was to remind them of his religion, the religion of peace.

"His sign was a true cross within a circle, my daughter, with the lines going out in equal directions from the center. It was not as the cross of the whites, symbolizing death. Instead it symbolizes life, and it looked much like this pendant which I have worn and which I now give you.

"The Pale One told our people that the circle represented all living things, and that the cross represented the center of the universe where each of us should stand. When a person stood at the center, the pale god explained, then no matter in which direction he turned, he was always looking outward at others. It was only when one left the center of the circle that he began looking inward, seeing only himself.

"To be truly happy, he told our people, they were to cease their warfare and begin to look upon their neighbors as they looked upon themselves. This is why we always blow the sacred smoke to the four directions before we speak in council. It tells everyone that our hearts are looking outward and that our words will be true, for we are not thinking of ourselves but only of them."

Ah, Milly interrupted,
I have respected this
ritual,
but until now I have not had
understanding.

"It is good that at last you do. My daughter, Giver-of-life has whispered to my heart that you are to carry this message of peace to all of our peoples. You will go as well to the nations of the whites, carrying the same message. Though young and a woman, you are mighty with words, and it is in my heart to tell you that many will hear you, and your life will do much good among the peoples of this land. Now, for tonight, I have spoken."

"But...but...my father," Milly pleaded, "I would know more of the pale god. I would know more of his teachings, of his religion."

"My daughter," the tall Seneca replied sadly, "I can tell you only this. For many seasons he walked among my people, doing good, teaching peace. Some say that when he left he walked alone into the west; some say that he arose into the western sky. I am not able to say, but this I do know. All of our people remember that he promised, one day, to return. In the long cycles of the dawn star since the Pale One walked among us, all else has been lost."

Andaggy's story fascinated me, yet it tore at me as well. Desperately I wanted to pursue it, for I longed, as had her grandmother, to know more of the pale god. Yet I dared not question further, at least for the moment. I had come to this Indian woman for other information, and that had to be paramount in my thinking no matter what else I might desire.

"But what of your grandmother?" I finally asked. "Did she accept the challenge? Did she continue to proclaim peace?"

"She did indeed, brother, and I will tell you of it. But let us first feed the hunger that is within our stomachs. My belly is growling as though it is midwinter and I am living through the season of famine. It is not a good feeling to have."

I grinned and nodded in agreement, though I was quite anxious to continue. More and more I was convinced that my sense of direction was correct, and that I had come to the right person.

"All right," I said with a sigh, "I too am ready to eat."

The Season
of Maturing

For the next few minutes, while I stood, stretched, and massaged the throbbing which was in my leg, Andaggy prepared a meal of ashcakes and jerked venison. I offered to help, but she would have none of it. I was her guest and would be treated as such. So while she worked I watched her and felt again the prickling sensations along my spine.

Andaggy was a small woman, and even though she was older, and was wearing men's clothing, she was still beautiful. Her movements were quick and decisive, her smile was always very near the surface, and her entire face seemed almost to glow with...well, joy was the best word I could think of. Everything about her made me feel that she was immensely happy, immensely contented.

But in addition to all of that, she looked extremely familiar to me. Though she was Indian, she looked in many ways like a white woman. Her cheekbones were high, of course, but her nose was thin, and her skin was very near the same color as my own. Of course, mine was darker than most, and with my black hair I had occasionally been called an Indian myself. It was, in fact, something that I had wondered about. The O'Connors had adopted me as a very small child, and I had one or two strange but very specific memories which, when I stopped to think of them, gave me pause. In fact, that was a part of what was troubling me about what Andaggy had said.

In the distant background of my memory, tiny and yet thoroughly familiar bells were ringing. It was as though the story which Andaggy was relating to me was more a repetition than an original telling. Yet that was hardly possible, and I knew it. Still, the prickling along my spine persisted, and I thought once more of my dreams.

They had not been elaborate experiences in the sense that great new things had been shown to me. In the first I had seen a woman, an old Indian woman who had been beckoning to me. She had been speaking, but I had no idea what it was that she was saying. In the second dream I had seen an Indian, his back to me, holding his hands upward in the attitude of prayer. In the dream I knew that I was acquainted with the Indian, but still I could not see him, could not learn his identity. In the third dream three men stood by my bed and spoke to me, three men who wore strange clothing, or at least clothing upon which strange markings had been made. Their message, which I remembered vividly, was what had sent me to find The Builder, the woman who now stood before me.

"Come," Andaggy said. "It is ready. Let us eat."

"Thank you," I replied. I sat beside her, and we both began.

After we had eaten, we cautiously made our way to the stream at the base of the hill. Though my leg pained me awfully, the cold water made the climb worthwhile. First Andaggy drank, and then while I did so she made a study of the tracks that were in the mud nearby.

"Brother," she whispered, as we crept back up the hill, "those tracks are fresh. The Americans who fired at me have not yet left us. We must be alert and speak quietly, for there is a great danger from these men who, though misled, are trying so hard to do right."

I nodded without speaking, sensing as I did a tightening within my throat, a fear that I might be prevented from learning what I had come so far to learn.

At last, seated beneath a large oak in the same secluded glen we had located earlier, Andaggy continued.

"Malcom O'Connor," she said, "I feel very strangely. All of my experience tells me to go, for I do not feel that it is safe here on the hill. Yet I cannot go, for something within my heart tells me to stay, tells me to continue, for you, the story of my grandmother. I do not understand this feeling which the Great One above has given me, but I will obey."

I too worried about our safety, but with all my heart I rejoiced that this woman felt impressed to continue her story. She did so immediately, and as she spoke her voice seemed filled with ever greater urgency.

"When the stranger had departed," she said, "my grandmother made a vow to declare his religion of peace wherever she went. And Hairy Man, though he did not fully understand her desires, did his best to encourage her along her difficult path. Nor was it many days, brother, before her road became truly difficult. Word of her message and of her zeal made its way from tribe to tribe, so that ere long she was more than well enough known. Some there were who accepted her and gave heed to her words of love. Others, however, made a mocking of her words, refused to trade with her husband, and scorned her and her children from their villages.

"They said, as they flailed her with branches and with stones, 'Ho! You do not know these things. You only repeat worn-out tales. Why should we love those who would hurt us? Why should we love those who would take our lands from us? Go to our enemies first, and when they are at peace with us, then we will be at peace with them. As long as they choose to hurt and destroy, we will *never* be at peace'."

"Their positions were well taken," I said, interrupting the Indian woman's telling. "It's a hard-found thing, finding love for a man who is trying to shoot you and take away your home."

"It is indeed, Malcom O'Connor. It is indeed. Until my grandmother understood this, until she learned to love even those who hated, she could not become the Peace Woman."

"Andaggy," I said slowly, thinking deeply about what I was saying, and doing my best to subdue the excitement in my voice, "as far as I know, such understanding and compassion come only after some severe trial. It is the nature of all mankind to learn best when we hurt most. Was that true of your grandmother? Was she hurt? or injured?"

"It was as you say, brother. She could not truly feel the words she was speaking until her pain became equal to them. That pain came to her in the thirty-third winter of her life, in the year of the white man 1723."

Hairy Man, Milly said, as they lay huddled together in the warmth of their fur bedding one cold January night,
this pale god
haunts
my every thought.
Wherever we travel
the tribes have
sayings of him,
and as I hear these tellings,
this god
and his message
become
more and more real
to me.
I long to live with gentleness
in my heart for
all others,
as I long for them to
accept me
and my children.
My husband, when do you—?

Suddenly, from outside of their small shelter, there came the startled barking of the dog, the braying of the mules, and above all, there were the horrid shouts of what sounded like demons straight from hell.

Hairy Man, leaping to his feet, picked up his musket and, pushing his sons and wife back down onto the sleeping robes, ducked through the doorway of the small shelter and into the darkness outside.

"You there!" Milly heard him shout. "Unhand those furs! Unhand those furs or I'll—"

There was a sudden explosion of gunfire, and Milly listened, horror-stricken, to the ragged choking of a dying man—a man she somehow knew was her husband.

"No!" she screamed as she crawled frantically toward the door. "No! I—"

And then, without warning, the bark covering was ripped from her shelter and she found herself staring into the angry faces of five white men. Instinctively she raised her hand in the ancient sign of peace. As she did, another musket exploded, she saw the flash of the gunpowder, and with that she knew no more.

Much later, hours perhaps, her head reeling and her stomach churning with nausea, Milly pulled herself to her knees. The snow where she had lain was dark with blood, and as she gingerly felt her head she realized that the blood was her own. The musket ball had struck her on the forehead and had cut a deep furrow along the side of her head, leaving her unconscious and apparently dead.

"Andaggy," I interrupted again, doing my best to ignore the constricting feeling which was suddenly building within my chest. "You say that she was wounded on the forehead?"

"Yes," the Indian woman said. "That is what I said. But—"

"Where was the wound?" I whispered. "I mean, on which side of her head?"

"On the right side, my brother, going from the hairline above her forehead down and back across her temple. But why do you—?"

"One thing more," I asked, certain now, but still fearful that I would be wrong. "Did the wound break, Andaggy, so that when it healed, the scar took the shape of a cross?"

Now it was Andaggy's turn to stare, to whisper. "But how...? How...? Ah, the dream! You know that from your dream! You must, for it is something of which I have never spoken. And yet you are right. It was as you have said."

"Ah, I had hoped it would be so," I replied. "And yes, you are right as well. It *was* the dream. In my first one I saw a woman, an old Indian woman, with a cross-shaped scar upon the right side of her forehead. She was holding her right hand in the air, beckoning to me, speaking as she did so. But Andaggy, I cannot remember what it was that she was saying. All I can recall is the feeling I had that I needed to find her."

In the silence which followed I stared at the ground and wondered if I should tell her the rest of it, the sense of memory which I seemed unable to avoid. It pervaded that first dream, it was there when I first met Andaggy, and it had been there throughout all of her narrative.

But no, it was a foolish thing I was feeling, not important enough to make mention of. Besides, the afternoon was passing, and more than ever I wanted to hear the rest of what Andaggy had to say.

"Is there more?" Andaggy asked, sounding almost breathless. "Is there more that you would tell me?"

"No," I replied quietly. "At least, there is nothing more that seems important to me. Perhaps later, when you are through..."

"Very well," Andaggy replied after a moment. "But should there be more, you must tell me. Giver-of-life has shown you the scar of my grandmother, and I would know of the reason behind his showing."

"As would I, Andaggy. As would I. Perhaps this day we will both learn."

"Yes," she replied. "Perhaps we will. But only if you will trust. But for now, back to the woman who became the seeker of peace."

Hairy Man? Milly called weakly.
My husband,
where are . . . ?

And then her eyes cleared and she saw, lying in the snow near her, the crumpled and very cold body of her husband. Gasping, she crawled to him and rolled him over. But there was no life, no warmth remaining in his body.

But what of her sons? she thought. Where were they? With mounting terror, Milly staggered to her feet and groped her way back to the cold ashes of the shelter. At first she found nothing, and hope rose within her like the sun on a frozen morning. But then, where a pile of furs still smouldered...

Oh, no! she cried out in anguish.
Please,
oh, Giver-of-life,
do not let
this thing
be!

But it was, for in the blackened embers of her lodge, Milly at last found the bodies of her two young sons. Each had been shot in the forehead, and both had been left to burn in the fire.

Ayieee! she screamed as she dropped to her knees, her soul filled with bitterness and hatred.

My husband,
I will avenge!
Ayiee,
my sons,
I will avenge!

And then, weeping, she collapsed onto her face in the ashes and the newly fallen snow.

Andaggy grew silent, and I could see that she felt deeply this long-ago experience. In the heat of the afternoon the birds around us had grown silent, and though the sun filtered down through the trees, and though the afternoon itself was beautiful, there was a somber, foreboding feeling in the air. The Builder, the woman who sat before me, had built even a mood into her telling. Her ability to show things with words truly was great.

At last, lifting her head, she gazed into my eyes.

"I am sorry, brother," she said emotionally. "I do not speak of this often, for the telling is hard, and I seem to live my grandmother's agony."

I did not know what to say, so I remained silent, hoping that she would be able to continue. At length she did, and I breathed a sigh of relief as I listened.

"Malcom O'Connor," she said, "who can know of the loneliness and sorrow of my grandmother? Who can know of the pain she endured during those cold days of mourning which followed? Who can tell of the hatred which built up within her heart toward the white murderers who had taken the lives of her family? It did not matter to her that the furs and trading goods had been taken. Nor did it matter that the animals too were gone. What mattered was that she had been stripped of her loved ones, and her heart shriveled and died as she made bitter plans for revenge.

"I do not know, brother, all that finally changed her heart. I know only that a strong thought came to her before she found the killers of her family. It was so strong that it brought back into her mind the mission of peace. The bloody scab on her forehead took the form of a cross, and it became, for her, the cross symbol which had been engraven in the hands of the ancient god. It was not until she had resolved once again to follow the ways of that god, Malcom O'Connor, that she found the camp of the robbers."

The wind, sweeping down off the snow-covered hills, swirled the white powder into miniature whirlwinds, small blizzards which rattled against the rocks surrounding the camp of George Black. Uneasily he turned from the fire and gazed off into the darkness of the night. The moon, a white sliver against the star-shrouded sky, was bathing the trunks of the winter-dead trees with an eerie, pale glow that gave them a spectral appearance. Black, the leader of a band of border ruffians, was almost unnerved by the soft sighing of the snow as it drifted through his camp.

"Lads," he said shakily, "hear ye that? 'Tis the devil's own footsteps walking about this night."

"Aye, that it is," agreed another, pulling himself closer to the fire. "'Tis the ghosts of those we have murdered, George Black, walking abroad to haunt us for our crimes."

"Bah!" sneered a third. "Captain, it be the snow we are hearing; the snow and nothing else! There be no such things as ghosts and devils. Nor do I relish hearing foolish tales concerning them."

"Aye, Cain," the large bearded leader finally agreed, as he turned back toward the fire. "Methinks you are right. 'Tis foolish for grown men to talk as we are. Dead men tell no tales; nor do they go walking abroad of a snowy, moonlit night. Nor woman nor young'uns either, I'm thinkin'."

"Cap'n," said another, obviously anxious to change the subject, "we've done right well this winter season, especially since we lifted the furs and the hair from that squawman trader."

There was a general chorus of laughter, and then another man spoke.

"Aye, Bill," he sneered, "we did well killing the man and the young'uns. But it was a shame that ye killed the squaw so quickly. She would have been a great comfort to all of us on long, cold nights such as this one be."

Again there was a chorus of murmured assent, and then for a time there was no sound but the crackling of the fire and the whisper of the wind.

George Black, deciding to retire, was just expressing that intent to his men when he saw, walking out of the trees toward him, the form of an Indian woman.

Cursing, he instinctively stepped backward.

"Boys," he whispered with a shudder, "I told you there was something out in those trees! Look ye yonder."

The men, springing to their feet, stared in awkward and frightened silence as the woman made her way out of the darkness, walking slowly toward the fire. Only when she stopped did those who were nearest to her recognize her.

"B...b...boys," one man stuttered, " 'tis the woman we murdered! 'Tis the ghost of the squaw come back to haunt us!"

There was a sudden, frightened intaking of breaths, and those closest to Milly made a mad scramble toward the far side of the circle to be nearer their companions.

Standing motionlessly, the Indian woman gazed evenly into the faces of each of the men, lingering only once as she looked deeply into the eyes of George Black, the man who carried her husband's scalp on his belt.

Brothers, she said quietly,
I raise my hand to you
in the sacred sign of
peace.
I show you the wound on
my forehead
for the same reason,
and to show that I am no spirit.
It is a wound undeserved but
well accepted.
I come to you in peace.

There was a subdued mumbling among the men, and one of them, the one who had refused to believe in ghosts, even raised his pistol as if to fire. But Milly simply stood there, unmoved by his actions, and after a moment the man lowered the pistol to his side.

You have taken our furs, she stated simply,

and have them piled here
behind you.
You have taken our animals,
and they now bray in the cold.
Though it pains me deeply,
I do not judge you for
these things.

    You have taken the life
of my husband,
and you now wear his scalp
on your belt.
You have taken the lives of
my sons—
you left their bodies
to burn
in the fire of my lodge.
In doing so you took,
as well,
my life,
leaving this shell to walk
alone.
I do not understand, but neither
do I condemn.

    Again Milly paused and gazed intently into the eyes of each of the men. In the fire a pocket of pitch, long imprisoned in a pine limb, suddenly burst. The men, startled, jumped as though they had been shot. Milly smiled without humor at their guilty reaction, and then she continued.

    Anciently, white brothers,
one with high soul-stature walked
among my people,
one with the cross of love engraven
in his hand.
Like you, his skin was pale.
Unlike you, he taught us love.

    He taught us that when
our brother
was in need

we were to give him
all we had.
     He taught us that when we were
offended
we were to forgive,
and to turn once more
to the
offender,
our hearts filled with
compassion and
love.
In that way, we would live his
peace religion.
     Brothers, you have taken
our furs.
I do not know why,
but I think that you must have been
in need.
You have taken our mules.
You must have been in great need.
You have taken the lives
of those I love.
Your needs must be
greater,
and far more strange,
than I can
understand.
     Brothers,
doing as the pale god
taught,
I now offer you more,
for your needs must be so much
that not even you
can understand.

Quickly, while the five murderers stared in open-mouthed amazement, Milly removed the bearskin robe which had, until that moment, protected her from the cold. It was burned along one edge, but other than that it had not been harmed by the fire. Folding it neatly, she placed the robe before them in the snow.

Brothers, she said, with a firm yet compassionate ring in her
voice,
this robe that is mine
give I to you.
All else that I have,
which is only my life,
now empty and alone,
waits before you,
offered freely.
Kill me now if you
choose.

Majestically she stood, gazing calmly from one to the other of
the men. And one by one their eyes dropped and they turned
away from her. At last, when no one moved, she smiled slightly,
raised her hand in her strange way, and once more spoke quietly.

Brothers,
hear now my words.
You have done wrong,
and it is strong within me to
punish.
Yet I will not,
for it is not the
higher way.
One day,
however,
Giver-of-life will see that you
feel of the agony
you have given
me.
Until that day,
remember this.
I am but one woman,
one footprint on the snow,
one shadow across the earth,
one wing against the sky,
one voice beneath the thunder.

Yet I am one footstep,
one wing,
one shadow,

one voice,
going forward!
To you, and to all people,
send I out, forever, the voice
of peace.

Turning then, and clothed only in her light deerskin dress, Milly vanished barefoot into the snowy darkness of the trees. It was—

"Malcom O'Connor." Andaggy interrupted her narrative as she held up her hand, "I hear the sound of horses and of metal. The militia are once more at the stream. Come with me quickly, and place your feet exactly where I place mine."

Silently she rose to her feet, scattered the few ashes from the fire, and moved rapidly into the trees. I followed, doing my best to move as quietly as she, and found myself hard-pressed, with my bad leg, to keep her in sight.

I could not recall when I had been so excited or so filled with fear. Andaggy's words had more than met my expectations, and it remained only to learn of the details before I would know for certain. Yet she was now moving in such a way that I could not tell if she planned to stop again or not, and I found myself worrying much about it.

I also worried about the militia, but there was nothing I could do about them, nothing at all. I even considered stopping, waiting for them, and revealing to them my identity. But that thought was short-lived, for there was no way that I could prove my citizenship. To them, I would be simply another British spy, another man to try and to execute with the greatest possible dispatch.

So, much as I longed to stop, to call back Andaggy and plead with her to begin again 'her narrative, I could not. Silence was imperative, as was distance, and I knew it. Therefore I followed without speaking, and I prayed that we would quickly reach a destination which The Builder would consider safe.

For some twenty minutes she fled forward, seeming scarcely to touch the ground, going from stones to dead logs to hard ground, avoiding leaves and grass and soft soil that would bear the marks of her passing. She obviously had a destination in mind, but neither of us spoke and I followed blindly, somehow certain that no matter what we did, the militia would not lose our trail.

"Brother," she suddenly whispered as we moved down the slope of a hill, "on that ridge yonder, hidden behind the trees, lies a cave. It is a place that was once sacred to my people, so no one but my people know of it. It is where we will hide, for though I should leave, I have yet much to tell you. What remains unsaid will go far toward furthering each of our missions for peace."

I nodded without replying, for we had moved so fast that I was short of breath. Additionally, my leg was causing me more grief than I could imagine, and I did not want her to see my weakness.

The Pennsylvania
Militia

The nine Americans, members of the Lancaster Battalion of the Pennsylvania Militia, squatted on the ground or stood by their horses, waiting. The Huron Indian was somewhere out in the trees, and though they weren't at all concerned with what happened to him, for none liked him, he did have the colonel with him, and they cared a whole lot about that. The colonel was one of their own, and they were going nowhere without him.

A boy, the youngest member of the company, squatted on his heels near the bank of the stream, idly tossing pebbles into the water. This was his first excursion with the group, and the excitement of it was fast wearing off. In fact, as he thought about it he realized that he was no longer excited at all. More accurately, he was troubled, and he was growing more troubled by the minute.

It had been the shooting that morning that had done it. That, and the evil intensity of the Huron. He had never known a man like the Indian, and he was frightened by him. Nor had he ever seen people who were as anxious to kill others as these men about him seemed to be. It went against everything his father had taught him.

He thought of his father as he picked up his new rifle and looked closely at it. A tool, his father had called the rifle as he had given it to the boy, no better and no worse than him who held it. And his father was right, the boy thought. The weapon could do so much good or it could do so much evil, depending upon who was firing it. In his hands, though, it would do good. He would be certain of that or he would never fire.

Picking up another rock, he tossed it gently into the stream. How he wished his father was there! How he wished his father was with them, taking control, using his mind to reason things out, showing the colonel that the Huron was evil and that something was terribly wrong with what they were attempting to do. Instead though, his father was off trying to rescue another American from the British, and the boy was alone.

Yet he knew how important his father's task of rescuing impressed American sailors was. After all, almost a dozen men had been spirited from British ships during the past year, and one of them had been his father's own childhood friend. That, though coincidental, had been very significant to his father, and the boy knew it.

He recalled then the storm of a few nights before, thought of the rescue he and his father had pulled off, and thought too of the old man named Malcom O'Connor whom they had saved. He was a strange one, that old man; quiet, and with his heart set firmly on helping to establish peace.

The boy had laughed at the idea then, knowing with all the wisdom of his youth that it could never be, saying proudly that he was glad they were at war with England, and stating even more proudly that he couldn't wait until *he* was able to fight. Both men had been shocked by his statements, for his father too had always been a man of peace. Later, away from the old man whom they had rescued, the boy had been severly reprimanded for his rudeness as well as for his attitude.

He was still bitter toward his father for that and had even refused to accompany him on his latest rescue mission. But now, as he thought about the apparently hasty and murderous way his company of militia had gone about trying to kill the Iroquois warrior, and as he thought about the hatred which seemed always to be gleaming in the eyes of the Huron, he found himself yearning more than ever for the company of his father, his father with his gentle, peaceful ways. How he wished now that the two old men would have had their way.

Peace would indeed be a wonderful thing, he suddenly realized, for there would be no need for mistrust, there would be no need for fear. None of them would be there by the stream looking for someone to kill, he would be beside his father working on the farm, and the Huron would be somewhere else entirely.

"Sam," he suddenly asked, as he hurled a small twig into the stream before him, "you understand the Huron's speech, don't you? What do you suppose he's looking for up on that hill?"

"Beats me, son," Sam replied caustically. "I may savvy their language somewhat, but I'm a far piece from understanding their thinking. Like I told the colonel before he went off with the Huron, there's something about this whole deal that smells. Trouble is, I can't track down the scent of what it is."

"But I don't understand," the boy responded.

"Neither do I, son. Neither do I. But I'll tell a man this much. There's more to this than one Iroquois spy, lots more."

"What do you mean, Sam?"

"Well, son, there's questions that I can't answer, and they trouble me somewhat. For instance, how did the Huron know where we could find that Iroquois brave this morning? I never got no official word, and I happen to know that the colonel didn't either. For that matter, who told us that the Iroquois was a spy? Nobody but the Huron. He's told us everything. And son, this man is one who doesn't trust that redskin. When I'm around him I feel about as nervous as a worm attending a convention of hungry robins. Nope, seems to me we're in the midst of something that's between redskins and redskins, and we're being used. This here Iroquois brave we've been chasing don't act like no British spy anyway. Near as I can tell, he ain't even armed."

"I agree," a third man said, speaking up. "Nobody, red or white, is foolish enough to stick around unarmed and wait for a musket ball in the brisket, especially when he knows an entire company of militia is after him. And that Iroquois brave knows!

He saw us, this morning. If that Indian is still around, then I'd lay a good wager that he isn't a spy."

"Well, then," asked another, "if you're so all-fired sure about this, why don't we just mount up and head back home? I've got a cow what's ready to drop her calf any minute, and she's never done it easy yet. I'd surely like to be there."

"I reckon you would, Aaron" Sam spat. "I reckon you would. So would we all! But if we leave this here bee-utiful location without a by-your-leave from the colonel, we'll all be facing a court-martial. Boys, I don't need one of them, not now or ever. I've got a family to support, and I reckon it'd be pretty difficult if I was in jail, or worse yet, shot dead. No, in this man's army I don't do nothing unless I'm told, and that's that!"

For a few moments there was no sound but the chuckling of the stream and the impatient foot-stomping of the horses. Then all at once the Huron was there, standing behind them.

All turned expectantly toward the Indian, but he stood silently without moving, a tall thin man with a stern visage which reminded them all of a hungry bird of prey.

The boy, shuddering, was the first to turn away from the Huron's stare, for the eyes seemed to bore into the boy's soul with such malicious evil that he could not bear it.

Slowly, as the Huron shifted his cold gaze to the others, they all dropped their eyes as well. Even Sam, last of all, turned away. At that the Huron laughed once, briefly, and then turned his back upon the group. He was standing thus when the colonel, out of breath and perspiring freely, strode into the clearing.

"Men," he gasped, "the Huron says there's two of them now. The Iroquois spy has been joined by someone else, but he can't tell if the other man is white or red. Whichever he is, the Huron figures they're both holed up around here somewheres. Given time, he'll find them."

"Colonel," Sam asked, spitting again, "you reckon this is something we ought to get mixed up in? Seems to me the Huron's got something of his own going here, and—"

"Sam," the colonel snapped, "are you questioning my authority? There's a war on, if you will remember, and the British will stoop as low as they must in order to win. You know how the Iroquois devils have plundered the frontier for the past sixty years

or so. Do you suppose that's all accidental? Of course it isn't!
Mark my words, they've done it all because they've been set to it
by the British. Why, left alone with us, we'd have the Iroquois and
all other Indians out of the way beyond the Mississippi. That way
they could do no more mischief against us, and we'd all be happy.

"Now, my orders are that you take an hour break for dinner.
Then we'll spread out, and by thunder, the boy here will have his
first British scalp before nightfall. Any questions?"

When there were none the colonel dropped his arm and,
turning, set about unpacking his mess. Quickly the rest of the men
followed suit, and none of them noticed the Huron as he lifted up
his musket, grinned evilly, and slipped silently into the trees.

The
Mighty Change

"My grandmother," Andaggy continued once we were in the well-hidden cave, and as though we had never been interrupted, "was still clothed only in her light summer dress when old Sheehays, the one who became my grandfather, found her. She was walking through the snow, not cold, and apparently unharmed by her experience with the white men. When Sheehays found her she seemed to be glowing with light, and she was holding her pendant and sending up a voice of gladness, chanting the strange peace chant she had learned from the tall Seneca warrior."

"How long had it been?" I asked. "How long had she been without her winter robe?"

"Brother, that I cannot say. One sun, perhaps two."

"But Andaggy, how...how did she keep from freezing to death?"

"Malcom O'Connor," the Indian woman answered, a slight smile working across her face, "there are two answers to your question. The first is the answer that I would give to a white man, which is that she must have found temporary shelter which protected her. The second answer would be given only to my people."

"Ah," I said. "Believers and unbelievers. We are back to the dreams, and to my white attitude."

"Yes, brother," Andaggy replied solemnly. "The white man is skeptical of all things which reason does not explain. To him, religion has created security, science has elevated theory, and the acquiring of wealth has eliminated faith. To master life, the white man says, one needs to apply reason; to obtain happiness one must avoid dilemma, throw away all mystery, and acquire wealth. So the white man says.

"Malcom O'Connor, my people do not believe this is so. Our religion has come to us from our ancestors. It comes through the dreams of our old people given them in the solemn hours of darkness by Giver-of-life. It also comes through visions to our wise men. All of these are written deeply within the hearts of our people and are followed strongly by all of us.

"Brother," Andaggy continued, "my people have a kinship with all the creatures of the earth, with the sky, and with the water. We are true brothers with all living things, and the earth is our mother, for she too is a giver of life.

"Brother, one goes out alone into the trees, into a clearing, and sits cross-legged in the thick grasses. The rim of the world rises immediately around him. The level of his eyes has dropped only a very little, yet he is much closer to the heart of the earth. In that way he becomes a part of the great quietness which lives and breathes about him. The winds, whispering through the grasses and the trees, are to him the voices of spirits which dwell in the earth. They are friends, and they can give much help to one whose mind knows such spirits exist.

"You see, Malcom O'Connor, when one understands how close my people are to the earth, then one has no need to ask how my grandmother survived. One knows, simply, that the spirits of her brothers the trees, the rocks, the wings, and the four-leggeds, watched over her. One knows too that her mother, the earth, nourished her and gave her warmth.

"But this is not all. In vision the pale god of peace sent out a voice to my grandmother; she heard, and was never again the same."

"She *saw* him?" I asked incredulously.

"Brother, she would never say more, for this was a sacred thing. The words I have spoken are all I know."

"Then tell me, Andaggy. How did she change? What made her different?"

"Ah, brother, that is a telling that I myself would wish to hear. I know but little, for as I said, I was but a very young maiden when she took the dark road of death. For my people the season of turning leaves is also the season of harvest and of giving thanks. Brother, the harvest season is the time of most good, for all growing things become mature and therefore can nourish their brothers. For my grandmother, this was to be her season of giving nourishment. It began when she walked out of the trees and into my grandfather's life. Come with me now to that morning."

To the seventh and last of the warriors running silently through the winter-dead trees, the day was beginning as the day before had begun, with more snow. The man had joined the Delawares on this rare winter raid, not because of his love for battle but because he believed the Wyandots had purposely wronged them and deserved to pay. It was therefore in his heart to take revenge. The small band of Indians were trotting single file along a trail that would later become known as Forbes Road, and at that moment they were climbing the eastern slope of the Allegheny Mountains.

The man, Sheehays, who was not a Delaware but was in fact a Susquehannock, had joined the war party when none of the other Susquehannock warriors would do so. For all time his people had been peace loving and friendly with their neighbors, both red and white, and he had determined to show them at last the way to true manhood.

Thus were his thoughts that winter morning when a slight noise caused him to glance away from the trail. For an instant he thought he saw a vision, but then he blinked and knew it was real. A young Indian woman, wearing only summer clothing, was standing in the snow watching him. And not only did she seem to ignore the cold, which in itself was surprising, but she seemed also to glow with an unearthly light, which was a thing unheard of.

"Brothers," he called softly but urgently to the Indians who were running before him. "Quickly, we must stop!"

Seconds later the group of seven warriors stood in the snow, staring in shocked disbelief at the young Indian woman.

"Kyunqueagoah?" Sheehays said as at last he recognized her. "How is it that you come to be in this place? And how is it that you come to be in such a pitiful condition?"

Brother, she replied quietly and gently,
it is a telling that is not important,
save to me,
for my family is
no more.
But it is good that you are here.
I greet the highest
in you.
Giver-of-life told me of
your coming,
and I now throw myself
on the arm of your kindness.

"Woman," the leader of the Delawares said caustically, "you will find no kindness here. Our faces are smeared with blood, and our hearts are hardened with the seeking of revenge. There is no place for a woman where we now go, especially one who is without sound mind."

"Shingas," Sheehays said with shocked surprise, "how is it that you speak in such a way to this woman? Know you not that she is honored, even as all women are honored among my people?"

"Bah! Then it is as I said before, Sheehays. No Susquehannock is a warrior! They all wear the petticoats of women."

For a moment the two men bristled at each other, and the tension among all of them was increasing rapidly. But suddenly the danger-charged silence was broken by the strangely powerful and yet very quiet voice of the woman.

Brothers, she said as she held her hands out toward them, her palms upward,
in the old days
our people had peace
within ourselves.
Even in times of cold
or of hardship,

when game was scarce and winters long,
we had peace within ourselves.
When others came against us,
destroying and killing,
that same peace was there,
very strong,
and we were happy.
    Yet you ask
how did we come by it?
My answer—
from our ancestors,
who were given the seed of peace
by the pale god who walked
among them.
    As our people went through life
that seed grew and grew
until it became like a solid tree
within us.
Our people could feel its branches
filling our veins
as we nourished its roots
with deeds of
kindness and
love.
No matter what happened to us,
we responded with love,
for our breasts were filled with
generous and
gentle hearts.
    This went on from season to season,
the tree of peace
all the time growing bigger
and bigger,
until the sap of
kindness
flowed thickly through the veins
of all our people.
    In our villages

no one was allowed to go hungry,
there was no disrespect
for the aged,
there was no enslaving
or abandoning of
children,
and the war trails became
pathways of brotherhood
and trade.

"Bah!" the Delaware leader scoffed, stamping his foot into the snow impatiently. "What is this that we are doing? Are we not men? Are we not warriors? How is it that we are listening to the words of a woman? How can she know of the true past, the true ways, of our people? Come, let us leave her as we found her. Let her tell the trees of the old ways. Perhaps they will be willing to listen. Perhaps the sap of peace runs in *their* veins."

For a moment there was silence, and the men shuffled their feet in awkward indecision. But Sheehays, who had long known the woman who stood before them, spoke.

"Brothers," he said, "I would hear more of the words of this woman. They ring true to my heart. Additionally, the Wyandots do not know of our coming, so there is time."

Turning then and acting as though the matter were resolved, Sheehays indicated that Milly should continue.

Now, brothers, she said, speaking as though she had not been interrupted,
all of that has changed.
There is little in the
way of
peace
which remains in the
hearts of
our people.
Perhaps it was the
coming of the
white man,
perhaps it was simply
a forgetting

of the teachings given us by
the pale god.
Whatever the reason,
the tree of peace which grew
within us
has withered and died.
Our bodies are now filled
with the dead limbs
of bitterness and
hatred,
and our veins flow freely
with the poison of
greed and
distrust.

Yet brothers, she continued with a note of finality,
the pale god,
he who came
with the dawn star,
has said that the
seed of peace
is still here.
Come,
let us return
to our people.
Let us forget the wrongs
which others have done.
Let us lift our thoughts high,
so that the seed of
peace
may once more grow into a
mighty tree
within us.
Brothers,
for this day
I have
spoken.

For a moment the warriors stood silent, without moving. But then Sheehays, with a decisive gesture, spoke.

"The woman is right," he said firmly. "My face is now turned in a strong manner toward where the sun rises. From this day forth I will no longer clap on the breechclout or raise the tomahawk against another. I too have spoken."

There was another moment's silence, then a Delaware brave stepped forward and spoke in the same manner. He was followed by another, and soon all had made the pledge except the one who had first spoken in a hard way toward the woman, the one called Shingas.

He stood there as his eyes bored into Milly's, but she did not waver, nor did she lose the peaceful look which filled her countenance, a look which seemed to say: "Forget your anger and your hatred. Come to me, for you are my brother, and my heart is filled with a great love and forgiveness for you."

Still he stared, his anger building, and Milly, unconsciously drawing her hair away from her face with her hand, smiled openly toward him, sending out her heart in peace.

For a moment the man seemed to waver, to hesitate. But then, with a savage grunt, he made a gesture of scorn toward the others, glowered at Milly, turned, and walked with a high head away into the trees.

"So then what?" I asked anxiously. "What happened next?"

"The Delaware warriors," Andaggy replied, "left Sheehays alone with my grandmother, and he returned with her to Conestoga Creek, to the home of their people.

"That first night, however, when the day had dropped behind the egg-shaped hills to the west, leaving dusk to flow into the valleys, my grandmother stepped in front of Sheehays, looked well into his eyes, and spoke."

Sheehays, Milly said, speaking quietly,
you have long been a man without
a woman.
Now I too am alone,
for Hairy Man and my children have taken the
dark road of no more sorrows to
the west.

One day past,
in the time of darkness,
the voice of Giver-of-life came into
my heart,
telling me that you would
come
to me.
You did,
and gave heed to the words of
my heart,
and now it is within me to say,
I would be your woman.

Sheehays, startled, stepped backward, covering his mouth with his hand in amazement. But as he looked more closely at the woman who stood before him, he saw that she was good to see. And then, somehow, he saw more than that, and his soul opened toward her.

"Woman," he said slowly, "this that you say is a mighty thing, and even now it is in me to turn away from your words. Yet within your eyes there is that which makes a man look twice, and then again. What you say is good, for I see that Giver-of-life means it to be. Let a voice be sent out to all people, from this day forth, that my heart has opened and closed fast upon the words of she who was known as Kyunqueagoah, but who will henceforth be known as the Woman of Peace. Today I take you for my wife. For now I, Sheehays, have spoken."

For a moment each gazed intently into the eyes of the other. At last Milly smiled, indicated that a shelter for the night was needed, turned, and strode quickly into the trees.

Soon the two, working together, were building a small wigwam. Milly was a woman of the people, and she would not allow either of them to rest until the shelter was up and ready for the first night's sleeping. First Sheehays cut young saplings which he and Milly planted firmly into the snow and frozen earth. Next the two of them pulled the saplings together and with cordage bound them into a round shape that was not round but only half round because it joined with the roundness of the earth to make it whole. With bark taken from dead trees they covered the structure, leaving the opening of the door facing the east because it was from that direction that the pale god would one day return.

When it was completed, Milly indicated to Sheehays that he should sit, for he could not help with inside work. It was her right as a woman to have things within her wigwam as she desired them, within the limits of tribal custom. She would not even allow Sheehays to help her make the fire, for it was also her right to kindle the flames which would cook the food and warm the lodge of her family.

In only minutes Milly had gone again into the woods and had returned, carrying two small pieces of wood and a strip of dried bark. In the center of the small lodge she knelt down on one knee, rubbed the bark between her hands into a shapeless mass, and placed it carefully on the ground. Then, putting her weight on her left knee, and using her right knee only to maintain balance, she began revolving a small stick rapidly back and forth between the palms of her hands. The pointed end of the stick spun rapidly in the hole of a flattened piece of softer wood which she had placed on the ground beneath the other. Soon a tiny wisp of smoke arose from the hole in the soft wood, and Milly smiled.

As Sheehays watched in silence, Milly revolved the stick even faster, and soon the smoke grew bigger. Suddenly she dropped the pointed stick, tapped the spark out of the flattened board and into the crushed bark, and gently lifted the mass of bark into the air above her. Softly and gently she blew up into the handful of dry tinder, fanning the spark with her quiet breath, nourishing it, helping it to grow.

Slowly the tiny flickering spread, and at length she lowered the bundle to the ground, placed tiny sticks upon it, nursed it, and soon had a bravely burning fire for the man called Sheehays, the man who had been sent by the Creator to take the place of her beloved Hairy Man.

Then, while the spirits of the trees whispered outside, telling Milly that they were pleased with her decision to take Sheehays into her life, she lay down beside him on the soft grasses which she had gathered from dry places to make into their bed.

Adjusting his robe to go both above and beneath both of them, Milly did her best to smile through the tears of loneliness and grief which suddenly filled her eyes. Though it did not feel right to have another husband, it was nevertheless as it should be. And Milly knew that, because she trusted Giver-of-life, her soul would one day be at peace. Smiling then she closed her eyes, whispered a chant of thanksgiving, and almost instantly dropped into a peaceful slumber.

In the days which followed, Milly learned that she had made a wise decision. Sheehays was a good man, the honored woman of her clan was filled with joy as she gave of her approval, and Milly herself was soon with child, which is to say that she too was filled with contentment and joy.

"Many seasons then passed," Andaggy continued, "seasons of joy and happiness in the lodge of my grandmother and grandfather. Nor am I able with words to describe what it was like. But build this scene in your mind, brother, as I use words to describe the land as the old ones, including the parents of my mother, saw it.

"These hills were our home, as far as the eye could see; from the great cloud-shrouded crests rubbing against the sky to the broad valley here where the great river runs, this land was for our use. These hills, with their much game and pure streams flowing everywhere, were home to us. We knew the trees as one brother knows another, the rocks were our friends, and the rivers gave us strength. We knew the meadows for their richness. We knew the animals by name. And always we watched the sky so that we could know the changing path of the sun.

"In the hills our wariors could hunt and trap, and in the fields along the rivers our women could grow the green corn and other seeds. The rivers gave us their fish, the soil gave us its strength, and the forest gave us its singing silence. To us, this land gave all that was necessary for life. We could not live away from it. We are as natural as water to this land. It has always been so. A spirit of my people will always be here, and a spirit of this place will be in me as long as I live, for I am a Susquehannock woman."

Again I dropped my gaze to the ground, for once more my throat was filled with a tightness that I could not yet explain. The sun was now dropping quickly toward the tops of the Alleghenies to the west of us, and yet there was still much that I needed to know. Andaggy must not stop yet.

"Is there more, Andaggy, that you could tell me about your grandmother and grandfather, Milly and Sheehays? I would know more of their efforts toward peace."

"Malcom O'Connor," she replied, smiling, "your spirit is strong, and my heart is warmed with your desires to learn of my grandmother's religion of peace. Until the sun reaches the tops of those trees yonder, or until the militia crosses the stream below, I will speak to you of it."

The Huron

In the afternoon sun there was no movement on the slope, none at all. Heat waves shimmered against the cloudless sky, and once a mockingbird gave voice from a distant chestnut tree. Other than that there was nothing, and this caused great confusion in the mind of the Huron.

Squinting the icy coldness of his dark eyes against the afternoon glare, he sat back and considered. The Iroquois woman, the one known as The Builder, must be on the opposite slope. He had tracked them carefully, she and the one who was now with her. Yet somehow the trail had vanished upon that hill.

True, the woman had left little sign, almost none at all except for the false trail, and the Huron, in spite of his burning hatred, was impressed. In fact, had it not been for the heaviness of the one who was with her, a heaviness caused because the man was in some way crippled and was unable to properly lift his leg, the Huron would not have been able to trail them even this far.

For a moment the Indian thought of the colonel and the other white soldiers, and he grinned maliciously. The colonel was soft like an old woman, as were most of the others, and in the Huron's mind he mocked them continually. Yet at times they had been useful to him. This day, he knew, had become one of those times.

The hatred which he felt for the woman known as The Builder was deep and abiding, a seething cancer which ate at his heart until he was consumed with thoughts of naught but her destruction.

Before his people the one called Andaggy had shamed him. With her soft words she had turned the hearts of the people of his village away from him. Because of the soft and foolish words of the one called The Builder the council of women had chosen another to be chief. They had chosen another when he alone had been qualified! Not one of them had been willing, from that day forth, to heed the words of strength and of war which he spoke. Instead, they now made a mocking of him. For that, he had vowed, the woman whose false voice had destroyed him, would die.

Yet for many seasons he had been unable to find her, unable to bring about her death. She was like a spirit, a will-o'-the-wisp, never in one place long, always vanishing before he could locate her.

But not many days before this, he had heard one white man ask another about her. The conversation had been quiet, hushed, but he had overheard enough to learn that she would be coming to the valley of the Susquehanna, dressed as an Iroquois brave, on this morning.

He had come immediately to the valley of the big river, and he had prepared well. He had long ago developed the skill of using whites against other whites, and he had used that skill now to the very best advantage, turning them against his mortal enemy.

He had told the colonel, the pompous fool, that Andaggy was a man, a dangerous spy, and that the spy's death would bring great honor to his militia. Always eager for glory, the colonel had ordered his men into the field without checking the Huron's story, and now their very numbers and their very clumsiness would help him locate the woman.

Still, the Huron was not anxious that the unsuspecting Americans kill the woman. He wanted that privilege for himself. In fact, he wanted it more than he had ever wanted anything. That was why he had left the militia behind at the stream. But now, having trailed her this far, he could not find her.

Angrily he slammed his fist against the ground. It was shameful that she, a mere woman, should outwit him. He was the Huron, the Quick Killer. Even his own people feared him, for he was master of all the deceits, the wiles, the skills of the greatest of the Huron warriors. That a *woman* should shame him and then outwit him was unthinkable.

Again he scanned the face of the opposite hill, his flat black eyes shifting rapidly from tree to rocky outcropping to clearing, back and forth across the hill, from top to bottom and then back up again.

In one place he saw a small herd of deer bedded down, waiting out the heat of the afternoon. In another he saw a place where a bear had been rooting for grubs in a dead log. But other than that there was nothing, no movement at all. It was as though she had utterly vanished from the face of the land. But that couldn't be.

And then, for just an instant, something flickered in the mind of the Huron, some indistinct memory of . . . of a sacred hill. Or perhaps it was something upon a hill, such as the one opposite him, which was sacred, something which concealed . . . But no, whatever it was would not come. He could not work the thought loose from his memory.

Again he searched the hillside with his chilling eyes, carefully, patiently. At last, with the sun dropping lower, he knew he could wait no longer. Not if she was to die, he couldn't.

Silently he rose to his feet, angrily he glared at the hill, swiftly he turned to go after the militia, and within seconds there was no sign of his passing.

Gently the wind whispered up the slope, shaking the leaves on the trees, sifting through the long grass, and gradually that beautiful day in May of 1814 prepared to bring itself to a close.

The Season of
Giving Nourishment

"Tellings, Malcom O'Connor. That is all this old woman who sits before you remembers. Tellings. Memories of memories told by another. Yet your quest is for truth, so perhaps these tellings will be of help to you.

"The Delaware braves who had been touched by the power of my grandmother's words spoke often of her. Soon her name became as a dry leaf before the winter wind, moving quickly from village to village.

"Here and there she was called upon to send out a voice for peace, and as she lifted her face and did so, many were touched by her words. And always my grandfather Sheehays was by her side, his eloquent silence lending much strength to her words.

"During the seasons of my mother's youth many nations of my people, the Shawnee, the Nanticoke, the Conoy, and the Southern Tutelo, were forced by the grasping fingers of the white man to settle in this valley. The Delaware too came here, building their villages northward along the great river.

"My grandmother did much to welcome these people and showed the way for the Susquehannocks, who were by then called the Conestogas, to open their hearts to the others. With the whites too my grandmother spoke peace, and often she took the Tulpehocken path which led to Philadelphia and to the leaders of your people.

"When the great man called William Penn took his long dark road to the west, the fathers of Pennsylvania changed their views toward our people. They feared the French in Canada, the six nations of the Iroquois seemed stronger than we, and so the white men declared the Iroquois, the Snake People, to be masters of all other Indian nations.

"This was not so, brother, but the whites wanted it to be. They hoped that by giving the Iroquois such power, the Snake People would defend the land of the Americans against the French. To some extent that is what happened, but it happened only a little.

"It became a time of great unrest among my people, for the Iroquois treated us as dogs, and made a mocking of our peaceful courage. Nor would the whites listen to our complaints. Worse, they too made a mocking, and appointed a drunkard and a fool to be the king over all the Delawares, a people who never before had known a king. They did this, brother, so they could control not only him but all the people they told him he ruled.

"Yet Sassoonan, for that was the king's name, being a man of weakness, was worked upon by others than the whites, certain men of his own people, who tore at him until he was like a wave, tossed to and fro in the wind. These men, tired of paying wampum tribute to the Iroquois, and disgusted with the worthless trinkets given Sassoonan by the whites, pestered him to go to war.

"Others there were who saw the futility of fighting, who desired the higher way of peace and brotherhood. It was in them to declare unto Sassoonan that a people were great only so long as their hearts were filled with great thoughts toward others, even others whose designs toward them were evil.

"These thoughts they shared, but the ears of Sassoonan at last were stopped, and he would not hear. He thought, finally, only of war. It was then, brother, that the Woman of Peace was called upon."

"*My husband?*" Milly asked quietly one evening.

Sheehays looked up from his task and caught his wife's gaze across the wigwam. The firelight danced across her face, causing her eyes to sparkle even more than they usually did, and he thought again of how good she was to see. Truly Giver-of-life, the Great One above, had been kind to him.

"Yes, woman?" he replied pleasantly.

For a moment Milly dropped her face, for she was ashamed of the words which were in her heart. Outside the winds of winter howled through the trees, and she knew that her desires were not worthy of a woman of the people. She must not impose unnecessary hardship, no matter how great the longing which was within her.

"Woman?" Sheehays asked again. "What is it which you would say?"

It is nothing, my husband.
It was a fleeting
thought,
one which even now has
drifted out with the
smoke from the
fire.

"Perhaps that is so," Sheehays said, smiling. "But woman, this man who sits before you would rather hear your thoughts which are nothing than the big thoughts of even the king who sits upon his wooden throne in England."

Milly giggled at that, and covered her mouth with her hand in even greater embarrassment.

"Come, woman," Sheehays urged. "Speak."

Milly gazed lovingly at her husband, certain that he would change his mind and turn away from her foolishness. But when he did not, she sighed and began.

My husband,
this new life which grows within
my belly
plagues me
daily.
I am swelling like a new squash,
and the child which is there will

most certainly be a
girl-child.

"How is that?" Sheehays asked, very interested. "How can you know such a thing?"

She pesters me daily, my husband,
with thoughts of
corn,
which is a woman's
thought.
Corn is all she thinks of,
and her thoughts fill
my heart until I cannot
rest.
Thus she will be a
girl.

Corn!
How I long for a meal of corn,
so that I can silence the
desire which this
girl-child has
given me!

"But woman," Sheehays responded, "do you not remember that it is the season of famine? I know of no corn in the entire village."

Ah, my husband,
that is so.
Only . . . only . . .

"Yes, woman? Speak."

Ah,
again it is nothing.
But I have heard that in the
valley of the
Ohio
the corn this past season grew
taller than the
trees,
with ears so big a
woman could carry only
two.

Ah, but the woman of the Ohio are greatly
blessed,
do you not think?

In the silence which followed, Sheehays dropped his gaze and stared at the earth, doing his best not to smile. A log popped in the fire and then settled, sending a tiny shower of sparks dancing into the air. Outside the wind howled more fiercely, and snow, drifting through the smoke-hole, sizzled as it touched the heated rocks which surrounded the fire. It was not a time for travel, and yet, for this woman...

"Very well," Sheehays said, as he rose to his feet. "For you, woman, and for Giver-of-life, who does not seem to have fed this girl-child enough corn, I will go to the Ohio."

Ayaii, Milly said with shocked surprise.
You would go,
my husband?
But no,
it is so far,
and—

"Hush, woman. It is only two days, three at the most, in each direction. It will be as nothing when placed alongside what you have given me."

Smiling then, Sheehays wrapped his heavy bearskin robe about himself, picked up his weapons, touched his wife upon the chin with his fingers, and was gone.

The next five days were the loneliest Milly had ever experienced. Almost every hour of each of the days she spent beading the design of her love onto a new shirt which her husband would proudly wear. And all night for each of the nights he was gone she lay alone, feeling the new life within her and fearful that Sheehays would be killed and never see his child.

On the sixth morning, however, Sheehays returned. He was walking, carrying his saddle and a small bag of corn for which he had traded his horse, and he was not alone.

The man who was with him, an elderly warrior from the village of Sassoonan, a village called Wyoming, requested of Sheehays that Milly go with him to send out the voice of peace to the foolish king. There was a brief discussion between Milly and

Sheehays, and soon the three were on their way to meet the puppet, the corn left uneaten in their wigwam.

The old man Sassoonan, Milly soon learned, was addicted to rum and false praise. Yet in council with him and a few others she spoke gently and politely. For half a day she unfolded to them the legend of the pale god, showing them how far the people had fallen from his teachings of peace.

At first there was much derision among the men, for this was a woman who spoke, and what could she know of strength? The people were weak, they told her, and could only become strong through war. Patiently though she taught them, and soon the eyes of their understanding were opened and they saw the way of true strength, true courage.

Brothers, she said finally,
we must honor peace
when it comes, for
too long have we been
comfortable
with war.
We must embrace our enemies,
for in them are our brothers born.
We can overcome our
weakness
only when our strengths
have all come
home
to our hearts.
Then we will be strong.

When she finished speaking, most within the council house arose; one at a time they clasped hands, and each in turn sent out a voice in prayer that the way of peace might fill their hearts forever. The others turned their backs in mocking and would not see the old ways.

"It was only then," Andaggy concluded, "upon her return to her own wigwam, that Milly got the corn she so desperately craved. And brother, the strangest thing of all was that by then the child within her, the one who was to be my mother, had changed her mind. The sight of the cooked corn made my grandmother nauseous, and she found herself, and so too the unborn child, craving a meal of roast duck."

We both laughed, and then Andaggy continued, still smiling.

"In the following season of growing, when the renewed grasses were bright and clear, when the new green of the fresh young leaves on the long-bare trees shone bright against the sky, and when the sun rose higher overhead, sparkling on the running ripples of the Susquehanna, Tenseedaagua came. She was a tiny girl-child, and she was sent by Giver-of-life to the wigwam of Sheehays and Milly not only to give brightness to their lives, but to become, one day, the mother of this woman who sits before you."

"What was her name again?" I asked her, doing my best to hide my mounting excitement.

"Tenseedaagua," Andaggy replied. "In your tongue she would be called the Little One Who Comes As a Gift, for to my grandmother she was a gift from Giver-of-life to ease her empty loneliness."

"And do you know what year it was that she was born?" I asked again, scarcely breathing.

"In the memory of my people it was the year of The Peace Woman. For your people it was 1728."

Dropping my eyes I nodded, hoping that Andaggy had not noticed the expression I was sure had been on my face. She must not notice, for it was not yet time.

Tenseedaagua, I thought. Was the name familiar, or was it that I wanted so badly for it to be familiar? I honestly couldn't tell, but I was getting closer to knowing. I was certain of that.

"It was to the white people," she continued, "that my grandmother made her greatest tellings. I will speak of them. The first I would say came to pass in the season of green growing corn, when the one who was to be my mother was still a very young maiden."

"But my mother," the girl pestered, as she hid behind her mother's skirt, "who is he?"

Hush, child, Milly scolded.

I have told you.

He is the son of
your uncle.

"But he is white, Mother. And he is not like the other boys. He hits nothing with the bow and arrow, the words he sends out are strange, he does not sit upon the ground as do our people, and—"

My child, Milly said, as she gently led the small girl down toward the river,
you do not understand.
His clothing is the clothing of the
whites
because they gave it
to him.
He and others have been to the
white school,
and—

"What is that word, my mother?"
School?
It is where one goes
to learn the ways of
one's people.
It is—

"Do *our* people have schools?"

For a moment or so Milly silently led the way down the pathway toward the river, uncertain of how best to answer her daughter.

Overhead the setting sun was building long streamers of cloud into fire, lighting the sky with endless shades of red, yellow, and violet. Past the cornfields, down on the river, a loon called out its plaintive cry, filling the silence of the early evening with a sense of lonely beauty. Out in the trees a whippoorwill called once, and then again. A squirrel above them scolded noisily as they passed, and a bee, a late worker, suddenly buzzed past, its flight a straight line that would lead, Milly knew, to its hive.

My daughter, she said, suddenly filled with understanding.
Our school is not as the
white man's,
in a building,
all closed in.

That is because our lives are not
lived closed in,
as they live theirs.
Our school is all about us.
The air,
the water,
the earth,
the two-leggeds,
the four-leggeds,
the wings,
and even the insect people
are our school.
It is the way of our people,
for we live in
the open.
For us,
it is a good way.

Much later, long after the others had fallen asleep, Milly lay awake, worrying. Her child Tenseedaagua was right, and Milly knew it. In just four seasons the boy who was her cousin had become almost as if he were not of the people at all. Nor were the others who had gone away to school any different. The things they had learned were good for the whites, but of what value were they to the People of the Falls, the Conestogas?

Others about her felt the same, and Milly knew it. Though they had been too polite to laugh and to ridicule, Milly had seen the shame in their eyes when the young men who had been away could not longer do as they had done before. Nor could her people speak of the sorrow they felt for these sons, for the commissioners of Maryland, Pennsylvania and Virginia were present, and it would be a shameful thing to show them of their hurt.

Yet it was there, and Milly knew it. She knew too that she had been chosen to speak to the commissioners upon the rising of the sun. These commissioners had asked for others of the young men to go east with them, again that they might be educated by the whites. But her people had decided against such a doing, and Milly must find a way of informing the commissioners without causing a breach between her people and them.

So Milly worried, and as she did so, the long night passed away, at last breaking into the soft gray of the dawn.

As the fingers of morning reached out before her, softly lighting her way, Milly moved silently away from the encampment and into the trees beyond. Upon reaching a small clearing, she stopped. Then, lifting her eyes and her hands upward, she began her chant of reverence and devotion. As she spoke, she thought again of the commissioners, and suddenly the words she must speak were given into her mind.

Thank you,
O Great One,
she concluded silently, smiling. Then, quickly, she made her way back to the village.

You have asked, brothers, she said later in council,
that we give a dozen of our
young men
to you,
to be educated in your colleges.
We are convinced that you mean
to do us good by
this thing,
and we thank you heartily.

But brothers,
in your great wisdom
you must know
that our life is
different
from yours,
and so our education must be
different as well.

Several of our young people
were formerly sent
to your colleges
and instructed in all of
your sciences.

But brothers,
upon their return
they were bad runners,

ignorant of every means of
living in the woods,
and fit to be neither hunters,
warriors,
nor counselors
to our young ones.
To us, they were
totally good for
nothing.
*   While we thank you, brothers,*
for your kind offer,
and though we decline
accepting it,
we wish to show our
gratitude
in this manner.
*   If you, great commissioners,*
will send us twelve of your sons
to keep while the snow falls,
and while the green corn grows and
is harvested,
we will take care of their
education.
We will instruct them in all we know,
and make true men
of them.
*   For now, I have*
spoken.

The Agony
of Lifting Others

As Andaggy and I laughed together, again I marveled, for the words of her grandmother displayed a delightful sense of humor, something I had not at all anticipated. I said as much to the Indian woman who sat before me, and her response was surprising and without hesitation.

"My brother," she said quietly, "laughter comes easily to all people who are happy. It was once so with my people. Laughter comes also to those who sorrow, but it is a shield, a mask, covering up the pain in their lives. Often it covers the pain from others, but usually it covers pain only for themselves, so that their sorrowing might be made bearable. This was so with my grandmother and her people; it is so with my people today."

In the silence which followed, a pebble broke loose and clattered down the rocks at the mouth of the cave. In one swift movement Andaggy was upon her feet, facing the entrance to the cavern. Her breathing was rapid, but other than that she appeared composed, ready. Yet nothing was there, and at last she turned to face me once again.

"You see, brother," she said, "how it is with those who live in fear? It is in my heart that I myself will soon take the dark road of death, the dark road which will bring an ending to my sorrow. In a way I fear this, but not for myself. As an old woman I am lonely, and I long to join those who have gone before me into the land of spirits.

"So, I do not fear death, not for me. I fear it only for my people. I fear, for when I am gone, who will send out the voice of peace? When I am gone, who is left to declare the way of the pale god? When I am gone, who is left to make a telling of the true way of my people? Who is left to tell them how it was when our warriors found strength in peace and honor in compassion?

"And so I laugh with you, brother. But in my heart I weep, for I know that the ways of my people are gone forever. My grandmother too understood this, sorrowed over it continually, and did all within her power to show the white man the good which lived in her people, hoping in that way to keep such good alive.

"At one time, when my mother was almost grown, the whites appointed one of their number to be an agent to our people. His duty, he thought, was to give his ways to us. My grandmother's duty, she felt, was to show him why her people could not easily accept such ways. With her words she did her best to teach him."

Brother, she said,
you wish our men
to become farmers.
But that is women's work,
for the men must do
other things.
There is order in this,
and honor.
    My husband says,
"You ask me to plow the earth.
Shall I take a knife
and tear
my mother's breast?
You ask me to gather harvest
from her.

Shall I, a man,
withdraw the child from
my mother's
womb?"
    No, brother,
these are woman things,
sacred to us,
and only bad will befall
our people
if men clap on
petticoats
and take them away
from us.
    Brother, to us
all things are
sacred,
including our mother the Earth,
and so all things must be done
in order,
including the taking of nourishment
from her breast.
    You say we must do business;
that all of us must work in the same way
to make a
living.
Yet if we make a living
in your way,
ignoring the sacred order of things,
then we lose our faces
and become instead only
images of what we were.
    Brother, for us
life must not
become
a business.

    "Those are noble words," I said, speaking carefully. "But
Andaggy, would it not have been easier if your people had gone

along with such men? It seems likely that you would not be ex-
periencing such difficulties as you are if your people had only
accepted the white man's ways."

"Perhaps you are right, brother," Andaggy responded gently.
"But tell me, which white man's ways were we to accept? Not
·many seasons past, brother, a band of Delawares accepted the
ways of the white Moravian missionaries. This included not only
the white religion, which was a whole-heart decision, but also all
the other ways of the whites. These Delawares became even more
than white, in all except their skin.

"Yet a black day came to the peaceful village of Gnadenhutten
when the American militia, under command of one David Wil-
liamson, descended upon the village, herded men, women, and
children into their church, allowed them to kiss each other farewell
and to sing "The Most High," and then promptly slaughtered
them.

"These people accepted the ways of the whites. Tell me,
brother, was it easier on them?

"To show further what I speak of, let me make another
telling."

The early-morning air was crisp and clear, filled almost to
overflowing with the sweet sounds of birds. The sun, not yet
visible, had painted the eastern sky a bright yellow, and the gentle
rolling hills of the Susquehannah Valley were awakening to
another day of beauty.

Atop one of these hills, her arms raised in reverence toward the
east, stood the woman Milly, the one who was known as the
Woman of Peace.

Her voice was rising in gladness, for she was sending out a
prayer, the chant of the god of the dawn. It was the same chant
which had been taught her by the old Seneca chieftain, a chant in
which she declared her devotion to the Pale One and promised to
await his return with eagerness.

Yet on that day all was not well. Milly's heart was in two
halves—one glad, the other a stone, heavy with sorrow. A white
Moravian missionary, Christian Frederick Post, had sent out the
voice of his religion to the people, and Milly was troubled.

Post was a good man, of that Milly was certain. His religion was good too, for he spoke of a religion of peace, and that was as it should be. Yet it was in Post's mind that neither Milly nor her people could have generous hearts, could have love for others, unless they became as he, white in all things. Milly had strongly disagreed with him, and the Moravian had departed, sorrowing for those he considered lost.

Now, days later, the event was still lingering in Milly's heart, heavy and oppressive. Something troubled her, something which she did not understand, and it was suddenly within her to speak with her husband of it.

Lowering her arms, she rubbed them against the chill of the dawn, turned, and was walking briskly down the hill when a twig snapped in the bushes to her side. Spinning around, she was surprised to see a British soldier standing there, his long pike pointed directly at her breast.

Startled, she stepped backward, and suddenly an arm was around her neck, her arms were jerked behind her, and within seconds she had been clapped in irons and was being forced away from her village.

Old Sheehays and the young woman, Tenseedaagua, anxious about Milly's delay, and hearing the noise of soldiers, arrived at the scene only in time to see Milly being thrown onto a horse. Sheehays, rushing forward, was knocked sprawling by one of the soldiers.

Tenseedaagua ran forward crying, a soldier stepped before her threateningly, Sheehays struggled to his knees, and another pointed a musket at him. Then Milly spoke, stopping all movement.

My husband,
my daughter,
be at peace in
your hearts.
All is well,
and in not many
days
this old woman will
return to the fire in
her wigwam.

Smiling then through the pain in her heart, Milly watched as

Tenseedaagua helped old Sheehays to his feet. Lifting her manacled hands in farewell, she at last turned away from her family, took hold of the pommel of the saddle, and started forward.

For two days the soldiers carried her eastward, mocking her and occasionally threatening her but otherwise doing her no harm. And for her part Milly was without complaint, sending out a voice of gladness whenever she could, smiling at the men always, and waiting.

Nor did she fear, for Giver-of-life had put it into her heart that all was well, and she did not doubt. Her heart was heavy only for Sheehays and her daughter, for they would worry, and that grieved her. Yet it was only a small grief, almost nothing compared to the joy which swelled within her when she thought of the way of peace, and of he who had declared it.

At last, in the afternoon of the third day, still in irons, Milly was brought into the imposing presence of Lord General Jeffrey Amherst, the English Governor-General of North America.

For several moments he ignored her, for he was busy with papers and could not be bothered by an old squaw. Finally he looked up, gazed absentmindedly in her direction, and then turned to one of the soldiers who had escorted her.

"Are you certain this is the one?"

The soldier answered smartly, told of her capture, and then became quiet.

Absently the man who was Governor General fingered a medal which hung about his neck, a medal given him personally by the king.

"Does she understand English?" he asked, at last breaking the silence.

"Remarkably well, sir."

"Well, well, well," he replied softly. "Imagine that! One of them may have a little intelligence."

Turning in his chair, he gazed out of the window, still fingering the medal which honored him for his efforts to peacefully unite the peoples of the colonies.

"Woman," he said, sounding bored as he spoke, "you have been accused of inciting your tribe against the British. How do you plead?"

I am known as Milly, she responded gently but quickly.
The name was given me by
one of your people,
who was also
my husband.
I give honor to the name,
as I do to your
people,
for they gave me
him.

When she stopped speaking, Amherst spun around and leaped
to his feet.

"What kind of an answer is that!" he shouted angrily. "You
filthy savages are all alike, talking in riddles and in circles, when
you talk at all. But *you* have no excuse! You speak the king's
English well enough. Now answer me plainly!

"Do you deny that you turned your pagan people against
Christianity? Do you deny that you turned your people against the
Moravian missionary Post? or against the agent we sent to teach
you farming? Oh yes, I know of that as well. You see, old woman,
your infamy is spreading. And do you deny, finally, that the
Indian devils have been murdering and raping throughout the
colonies, all under your direction?"

Milly, surprised at his outburst and his accusations, still said
nothing. In her mind, though, was a memory, a telling given her
by a white trader, and as she thought of it her heart grew cold.

This man, the one with the medal of peace hanging upon his
breast, was the one who had been responsible for sending the
smallpox among her people at Fort Pitt.

As she thought of this Milly could still see in her mind the
portion of the letter, sent from Amherst to Colonel Bouquet, in
which he had encouraged the colonel to spread the dreaded disease
among the Indians.

> You will do well to try to inoculate the Indians
> by means of infected blankets, as well as to try
> every other method that can serve to extirpate
> this execrable race.

Now, as Milly recalled the horror she had felt upon reading the
letter, she felt the first trembling of fear. No matter what she said,

she suddenly realized, the man would not listen. It would do no good to explain, to plead, or to attempt to teach. The man's heart was a rock, his hatred was firm.

Slap!

Milly's head rocked backward with the force of the governor general's open-handed blow.

"Nobody ignores me when I speak," Amherst snarled venomously! Now I will ask you only once more. What say you to the charges?"

Brother, Milly answered gently, ignoring the pain which had spread across her face,
you have demanded that
this old woman,
who in strength is as nothing
next to you,
should speak.
Hear now the
truthful
words of her
heart.

For me, I deny
nothing.
For my people, I deny
all.

We, the Susquehannocks,
are a people of
peace.
Since first Captain Smith came to
our villages,
or since William Penn signed the
first great treaty with
our fathers,
we have not lifted the
hatchet against the
whites.
Nor will we,
no matter the course of
others.

*For my brothers of the
other nations of
my people
I cannot speak.
Still, I know their
hearts,
and would make a telling
of that.
    Though most of my people desire peace,
there is no way
to live peacefully
beside you.
Why?
Because you judge the order
of our life
to be childish
and savage
while you yourself live
lower than the
four-leggeds of the
forest.*

Amherst's face grew livid with anger, and he was about to strike Milly again when she held her iron-bound hands up before her, stopping him.

Do you question my words? she asked quietly.
*Think long thoughts,
brother.
Think of the letter to
Fort Pitt.
Think of the blankets
filled with the
smallpox sickness,
given by your order to
my people.*

Amherst reacted as though struck. The blood drained from his face, his hand reached for his throat, and he found himself gasping as though he could not get enough air. How could she have known of that, he wondered frantically? There was no way, no way at all.

There is more, Milly continued, her voice rising slightly.
You charge that we are not
religious,
yet of all people we are
most so.
But you do not understand
our prayers.
You do not try to understand.
Without understanding,
you condemn us as lost souls
simply because our form of
worship
is different than
yours.
Brother,
if your religion is filled with
such good,
why are you so consumed with
hatred?
If your religion is filled with
such good,
why do you differ so
with others of your people
about it?
You say your religion was
given to you by your
forefathers,
and handed down
from father to son.
Our religion came to us in
the same way.
The difference is that, while your religion
came from a book,
ours came from a pale god who
once walked among us.
You quarrel with others
over what is in your book.
We do not dispute among ourselves

concerning the words of
the pale god.
    He told us to be thankful for what
we receive,
to love each other,
and to be united as
families and as
people.
When we do this we walk
in beauty,
with gentleness in our hearts.
    In truth, brother,
we do this
gladly.
Is this not a good religion?
    We do not wish to
destroy
your beliefs.
We desire only to live
our own.
Yet we cannot, for
your people come as the floods
in spring,
with no stopping,
mocking us and condemning us for
what we do,
even killing us
wantonly.
    Brother,
the ways of our people do not
come together.
Perhaps it is best that
we live apart.
Forbear settling our lands
across the Allegheny hills.
Call your people back to
this side,
lest more damage be done and

you think greater ill
of us.
    If the medal about your neck is true,
then take the rum from
your traders.
It brings no good to
my people.
Let them give us instead
valuable goods for
our furs,
lest both we and they be
ruined.
    Brother,
our people
are filled
with the tree of peace,
a tree which one day
must give
shade
and protection
to all mankind.
We do not desire to take up
the hatchet
nor clap on the breechclout of war.
We desire only peace between
our peoples.
Perhaps, my brother,
if you watch closely,
you will learn,
from us,
the higher way.

When Milly finished speaking, Lord General Jeffrey Amherst said nothing, but in his pale eyes there burned a hatred which was a deep and evil thing. For several seconds he simply glared at her, doing his best to make her drop her eyes. When she didn't waver he turned away, pulled himself to his full height, clasped his hands behind his back, and spoke.

"Woman," he said harshly, his voice seething with anger. "I find you guilty of all charges!

"Sergeant, hold this woman in irons, secured tightly, until daylight. Then hang her by the neck until she is dead. That is all. Take her away."

In the guardhouse, a stout structure of hewn logs with no windows save a small one in the door, Milly sat quietly against the wall. Outside the two guards were laughing loudly as they finished off their meal of beans and coffee. When they were through, the door opened and both men entered. One of them unlocked the irons on her wrists, pulled her hands behind her back, and locked them there. The other, the sergeant, checked the irons on her legs and then for good measure bound them further with a rope which he secured around her neck and then to a beam in the ceiling.

"There," he said at last, grinning. "That'll hold the wench until morning. Might even save us the trouble of hanging her."

When he had gone, the second guard, who had lingered behind, suddenly spoke.

"Ma'am," he said softly, "were you on the Upper Sandusky a year ago?"

When Milly nodded, the guard continued.

"As was I. You found us the night our raft overturned in the rapids. I'd have frozen that night if you hadn't been there to make a fire and feed us."

I remember, Milly replied, smiling up at him.
It was indeed a
time of great
cold
and hunger.

"I'd tell a man it was! But anyway, ma'am, I reckon you'll be a mite hungry your ownself about now. I'd be beholden if you'd let me fetch you a bit of food."

Thank you, Milly said, her voice filled with sudden emotion.
But on this evening
I have no
need
for nourishment.

"No, I reckon you don't. Well, at least I'll loosen this rope a bit . . . There! The sergeant had no need to do it this tight. I suppose he wasn't thinking clearly. Is that a little more comfortable, ma'am?"

Milly nodded, smiled her appreciation, and dropped her eyes as the unexpected friend turned to leave. But he stopped, turned back as if he had forgotten something, and spoke again, very quietly.

"Ma'am," he whispered, "I'm awful sorry about how the general treated you. No man ought to treat a woman in such a manner. I'm sorry too that you were sentenced to hang. He'd no call to impose such a sentence. Trouble is, he's a mean and evil man, one who loves to see the suffering in others."

For an instant the guard paused, looked about him to be certain they were alone, and then continued, speaking quietly and rapidly.

"I've thought on it, ma'am, and I don't see any way I can get you out of this. But you must know that I will not stand by and see you hung. I will find a way to get you out, and—"

Brother, Milly said kindly,
do not be
concerned.
Giver-of-life
is with me,
and all is well.

"Uh . . . well . . ." the man stammered, confused. "Uh . . . I don't know anything about that there, ma'am. But still, I will do what I can! I promise!"

Turning then he strode quickly from the guardhouse, closed the door, locked it, and was immediately confronted by the sergeant.

"Getting a mite friendly with that squaw, aren't you?"

"I'd like to be, sergeant," the man replied. "She once saved my life. It's a shame for her to go this way."

"Not to my way of thinking, it isn't. Any dead redskin is better than a live one. Now hand over those keys, lest your *humanitarian* heart overcomes your better judgment."

Slowly the guard handed his superior the ring of keys. The sergeant quickly looped about his neck the string upon which the keys were hung, and then he tucked the brass ring of keys down inside his waistcoat.

"There," he said, grinning. "That ought to keep them safe until we swing her in the morning. Now come with me to the fire, where you'll take first watch."

Deeply disappointed, and yet still filled with hope, the second guard did as he was told. One way or another, he told himself. One way or another.

A little later, when it was not quite dark yet not quite light, Milly lifted her face and sent her voice toward the ceiling. She spoke out loud but very softly, and her words were in the ancient language of her people.

Ho, Great One above,
Ho, you who walked among my people,
Ho, you who taught peace.
    Hear the voice I send out,
    Hear the plea I am sending.
    Come down now.
    Come down now if it is good.
    Go into the hearts of those men,
        those men who think evil.
    Help them feel of goodness,
        or help them sleep,
        whichever seems best
        to you.
Ho, O Great One,
    This woman who would serve,
        gives thanks.

Bending her head downward then, Milly closed her eyes, relaxed as best she could, and waited.

Outside where the guards watched, firelight flickered on the under-branches of the surrounding trees and reflected from the smooth face of the log guardhouse. The air was still and silent, and the fire crackled and popped as it ate the dried wood which the guards occasionally fed it.

Off in the trees a quail called, and from far away a lone wolf lifted its immeasurably lonely voice toward the starlit sky. Both men glanced uneasily out into the darkness and then at each other. Neither spoke, but each knew the squeamishness the other was feeling.

Much later the guard who was awake and actively plotting

Milly's escape noticed a strange pale glow coming from the tiny guardhouse window. Momentarily he wavered, but then, concerned about Milly's safety, he awoke his superior and pointed it out to him.

For a moment or so the two sat together, wondering. Then the sergeant thought he heard voices coming from within the guardhouse. Alarmed, he rose to his feet to check, took hold of the keys in his waistcoat just in case, and his next awareness was of the early morning sun warming his face.

Anxiously he leaped to his feet, awoke the other guard, and then with relief noted that they were still alone. At least the governor general had not yet arrived.

Leading out, the sergeant sprinted toward the guardhouse door, which he found still locked, barred, and exactly as he had left it.

"Here!" he shouted in frustration. "Take these keys and open the door, blast it all!"

The other guard, fumbling with the key and cursing himself for sleeping while he should have been finding a way to free the woman, at last opened the lock, swung back the door, and stared in shocked disbelief at the empty room.

With halting steps the two men entered, moving cautiously toward where Milly had been secured. The irons, which had covered both her wrists and her ankles, were lying on the floor, still locked. The rope which had bound her legs to her neck, and had gone from there to the beam above, still hung suspended, the knots exactly as the sergeant had tied them. Nothing was changed, nothing except that their prisoner was gone.

"It's not possible," the sergeant muttered. "It just can't be so."

"I agree," the other responded, almost in a whisper. "But sergeant, that was no ordinary woman, either. She's something special. She's the one they call the Peace Woman. With her, I'd believe most anything."

The Season of
Cold Sleeping

"But how," I questioned, ". . . how—?"

"Brother," Andaggy chided gently, "do you still doubt? Is this telling any different from your dreams? You should not question how, but why."

"I don't need to question why," I replied uneasily. "I think I know why. She obviously had something left to do. But how can a man who is trained in reason—?"

"Malcom O'Connor," the woman interrupted, "reason regarding spiritual things is usually faulty because we two-leggeds have not been given adequate information. Had we been given all knowledge, all spiritual dilemmas would become wonderfully clear."

For a moment I nodded my head, chuckling. "And so The Builder," I said, "the woman who saved my life, is also a philosopher."

Andaggy smiled modestly, and I continued.

"One day, Andaggy, you must share your views with Thomas Jefferson. He would be most interested in them."

In the moment of silence which followed, I eased myself into a new position on the rock. The cave was damp, and the chill had worked into my leg so that it was throbbing like a dozen toothaches. Unconsciously I kneaded it with my fingers, not consciously thinking about it, but running over in my mind Andaggy's latest telling.

"Your leg troubles you greatly, Malcom O'Connor. What is the cause of the pain?"

Embarrassed that she should have seen my weakness, I looked away and spoke.

"It is the gout," I said simply. "For years it was in my foot, but now it seems to have moved higher. Comes as a result of my years at sea, I suppose."

"Perhaps," Andaggy said hopefully, "if there is time, I can gather a few herbs, and—"

"Andaggy, you're wonderful to think of such a thing, but I'm fine. Really I am. Besides, I would much rather spend what time there is left in listening to you. Now, let us return to your grandmother. What was it that she had remaining to do?"

"Men," Andaggy said scornfully. "You're all alike, so afraid to show what another might consider weakness. But very well, I shall say no more about your suffering. Come back with me, then, and you will see."

"Old Woman," Sheehays said, as they shared the warmth of the nighttime fire, "it would seem that the Delaware captain, Shingas, does not care for your words of peace any more than did the governor general."

The old woman, Milly, who was now called always the Peace Woman, nodded her head sadly in agreement.

That is so, my husband, she said quietly.
Shingas has not changed since the
day you ran with him upon the
warpath,
the day you found me.
He would not turn away
because of my words
that day,
nor will he turn away

because of them
now.
His heart has turned to
stone,
as did the heart of Lord Amherst.
But while the governor general's heart
hardened
with anger,
Shingas's is heavy with sadness for
his people,
cold with the knowledge
that no treaty will keep the whites from
our lands,
and hard with the determination
to resist them
as long as he lives
and breathes.

Slowly she stood up and, with aching limbs, moved to pick up the pot of corn mush which was their evening meal.

"I myself feel the thoughts of his heart," Old Sheehays said sadly. "They are hard thoughts."

Yes, they are,
my husband.
Ere long this land,
which has been home to our
people
for so many long cycles
of the
dawn star,
will be but a memory.
The springs of awakening,
the summers of rejoicing,
the autumns of hunting,
and the winters of
teaching our children
will be gone.
It has been taken
from us
by one man's cleverness,

another man's dishonesty,
and another's lack of concern.
It has been measured and
cut up and
sold
until the whole of it
is worn out and
sick.
*   Yes, my husband,*
I too understand the
thoughts
of Shingas's heart.
*   Yet within this old breast*
swells the
certainty
that such greed will never
stop
until all people can stand
in the center
of the true cross,
looking outward instead of inward,
becoming one in
brotherhood,
resting in the shade
of the great tree of
peace.
This movement must be
even as the pale god
said it would be—
small at first,
yet growing always
larger.
*   My husband,*
it must start
with me.
This I have been
told.

Old Sheehays sighed deeply as he gazed with affection upward toward the age-lined face of his companion.

"And so always there has been peace within our wigwam, Old Woman. Because of you it has been good."

Milly smiled modestly but said nothing, and so Old Sheehays continued.

"Then on the morrow, Old Woman, you would continue your journey to the Monongahela, to Fort Duquesne? You will not rest?"

No, she said after a moment, shaking her head with determination.
If my people will not
listen
to me,
then perhaps the French
and the English
will hear my words.
One hopes that my voice will
prevent them
from playing with the
lives
of our people
as they make war over the
ownership of
our lands.

For a moment the old woman paused, looking down at the wrinkled old warrior who was her husband. Then she smiled and spoke.

Now join me beneath the blankets,
Old Man.
This bag of bones
is cold,
and no fire can
warm me
as well as
you.

"Ungh," Old Sheehays grunted, smiling in return. "That is good. Come here, then, and let the warmth begin."

Laughing in unison, the old couple snuggled together beneath their robes, ignoring the darkness of age that was crowding closely upon them.

"She was quite a woman, that grandmother of yours," I said, grinning widely.

"Yes," Andaggy replied, "she was indeed."

"And did it work?" I asked. "Did her mission of peace to the French and to the English ever accomplish anything?"

"How does one know, Malcom O'Connor? Perhaps she touched the heart of someone here or someone there. One would hope that she did. Yet that was the beginning of the winter of her life, the season when nothing moves, for the great leaders gave no heed to her words, and to her sorrow the blood-letting on our land grew ever greater.

"Shingas became known among the whites as Shingas the Terrible. Teedyuskung, another Delaware, did much damage here in the valley of the Susquehannah, and Governor Robert Morris of Pennsylvania declared war on our people in 1754, offering cash bounties for all Indian scalps taken. It was the beginning of what has come to be known as the French and Indian War.

"For my people, however, the People of the Falls, the war made little difference. There were few of us left, not more than two dozen on the whole face of the land. Yet under the direction of the Peace Woman we did our best to be happy, to keep our hearts strong and straight.

"Despite the wars which raged around our village on Conestoga Creek, my people had become known to most of our white neighbors as the People of Peace. Though I was but a child, I remember visiting in the homes of many white friends, selling to them the baskets, brooms, and bowls which my people manufactured in our village. In fact, it is in my memory that on a long ago day I went with my father, who was called Chee-na-wan, my mother, Tenseedaagua, and my younger brother, Connoodaghtoh, to the home of some people called O'Connor. In fact, brother, it is in my memory that these O'Connors lived at Donegal Springs. Was this *your* family, brother?"

Quickly, before Andaggy could see the tears in my eyes, I turned my head and gazed back into the darkness of the cave.

"Was there . . . was there a little girl, with hair the color of bright corn silk, Andaggy? And did she . . . did she give to you and to your brother a sweet which she called blackstrap molasses?"

"Ho!" the woman exclaimed, visibly excited. "You *were* there, brother!"

"Yes, Andaggy," I replied with deep feeling. "I was there. I . . . I remember you, as I remember your father, your mother, and your . . . your brothers."

"Ahh!" Andaggy was obviously relieved. "That is why your face has the seen-before look which has troubled me since this morning."

Again I nodded, and though I wanted to speak, to tell her all that was tumbling forward out of my forgotten past, filling me with memories and with understanding, I could not, for there was no strength in my voice. Yet I had been there. I had! I could remember it.

"Malcom O'Connor, there is yet a final telling that I would make before we take our separate paths. Would you hear me out?"

"Aye, sister," I said emotionally, "I would listen."

"In the white man's year of 1758," Andaggy began, "Christian Frederick Post, the missionary I mentioned earlier, promised my people that the white men would be kept east of the Allegheny Mountains. One winter later George Croghan, the colonial deputy Indian agent, made the same promise. These men were sincere in their words, but both later realized that neither they nor the white government could control the westward reachings of the white people.

"In 1763, a great Ottawa chief, whose name was Pontiac, declared war against the encroaching whites. For that entire year the tributaries of the Susquehannah ran red with blood. Once more my people remained at peace, though Pontiac was not pleased by our decision, and made many threats against us. Yet there were white men around us too who would not accept our peaceful desires. These men sought the scalps of all my people, friendly or not, for their bounties.

"My grandmother must have been told by Giver-of-life of what was to come, for she did all she could do to prepare us for it.

"Early in the last month of that year, while she and I were in the woods gathering up what few nuts our brothers the squirrels had left, she spoke to me like this:

My daughter who is the daughter of

my daughter,
a long time has this old woman
lived with you.
But soon we must be going
separately
that we may be
together.
Do not be sad, for this is a
happy thing,
and I will continue to do you
much good.
Be a woman of great goodness
within the heart,
accustomed to small praise
for honesty,
and do not work for the sake
of attainment.
That must not be the way of
the People.
With your husband, feed and shelter all
who enter your lodge.
Protect but never
possess them.
Build a lodge of
solid thoughts,
a fortress of
introspection.
Do not be afraid
of silence,
for that is the
voice of
Giver-of-life.
If you listen,
he will teach you self-control,
endurance which is true courage,
patience,
dignity, and
reverence.
Silence, my daughter,

*will teach you
womanhood.
    Now, remember.
Watch for this old woman and
she will be
seen.
    Perhaps she shall be
the wind
to ruffle the water
so that you do not see your
beautiful face too much
and become vain and proud.
    Perhaps she shall be a
star
in the star nations above,
guiding your uncertain footsteps
so that you have
direction
in the darkness.
    Perhaps she shall be
the rain,
softening the earth
so that the seeds of your life will find
nourishment.
    Perhaps she shall be
the snow,
covering your lodge
with her soft blanket
of cold
so that your blossoms will increase with
each new season of life.
    Perhaps she shall be
the stream,
singing and dancing
across the stones of your years
so that you are never without music
in your heart.
    My daughter,
whatever she will be,*

this old woman who is now
your grandmother
sends out her voice to you,
and places the mission of peace upon
your heart.
It is yours as it was hers,
for you alone are left
to carry it.
Hear the words of this old woman,
for they are strong,
and you must be strong to
bear them.
See the scar on this old forehead,
the scar of the cross,
and remember;
from where the sun now stands
you must be,
even as she has been,
a seeker of
peace.
*   For this day,*
and forever,
this old woman has
spoken.

The Dark Road

"The words of your grandmother touch me deeply, Andaggy. They must be of great comfort to you."

For a moment the Indian woman looked away. She said nothing, but her fingers, long and slender, worked nervously with the fringe on her beaded shirt, and I was certain that she was agitated. Suddenly she spun around to face me, and I was taken back by the intensity of her voice.

"Yes, Malcom O'Connor," she said, with deep feeling, "the words of the Peace Woman were great. But I, a mere child, gave no heed. Nor did I give heed until Giver-of-life, two times, took my family from me. Only then, when such pain was forced upon me, did my heart accept the charge. Only then did I become a seeker of peace. But . . . but it was too late, and I have done no good! No one is willing to hear my words, and I grow weary, yes, and fearful too, for I have not convinced many of the true way. To the contrary, I have turned many against me, so that their hatred is even greater than before. Nor do I blame them. Though in my heart I know that the way of peace is the high way, my reason tells me that one must fight to protect what one loves and what one believes. How can any of us, red man or white man, do otherwise? Oh, my brother, what is an old woman to do?"

For almost a minute there was silence, undisturbed. Then the woman, her voice filled with resignation, spoke again.

"But enough of me, Malcom O'Connor. Enough of the complainings of an old bag of bones. Let me hear now of you, of your dreams, and of your own quest. I hope you have been more successful."

Nodding silently I shifted slightly on the rock to ease my leg again, and then I began. And as I spoke, telling the Indian woman of my boyhood, the afternoon light continued to creep across the floor of the cave toward us. The day indeed was fast ending.

"And so," I said finally, "when my wife died of bilious fever, having never borne a child, I began wandering about the land, seeking some reason for my existence. The Holy Bible proved to be of great comfort to me, and I read it constantly. I must admit, though, Andaggy, that I became a sect by myself, for it seemed clear to me that many of its teachings had been distorted. In fact, I feel precisely as does our recently retired president, Thomas Jefferson, who is even now compiling his own bible from what he considers to be the few accurately recorded teachings of Christ. When last I visited with him at Monticello, he had snipped and cut his way through three of the four gospels."

"Brother," Andaggy interrupted, "I have often thought the same thing regarding your Bible. I read much from it during my schooling among the whites, and often it seemed contradictory."

"Yes," I replied, "a great many people feel that way. But now to my dreams, the first of which occurred when I was praying to be relieved of thoughts of murder which I harbored toward the brutal first mate of my ship."

"In that dream," Andaggy said, interrupting me, "you saw my grandmother, who was the Peace Woman. This is from the Great One above, and my heart tells me it is true. I look forward to hearing of the others."

"I saw in my second dream," I said eagerly, "another Indian. This one, however, was turned away so that I could see only his back. His arms were in the air, perhaps chanting a prayer, and I somehow knew that he had been building something, or was a builder."

"You saw *me*, my brother? Is this what you are saying?"

"Yes, Andaggy, I believe I did. At first I was far from certain, for I thought I had seen a man. Yet as we have visited this day . . . Yes, I'm certain it was you I was shown."

Solemnly Andaggy nodded. "This that you have spoken is good, brother. Giver-of-life speaks in dreams to those who will listen. My heart says that he has spoken to you, though still I do not understand why."

"I believe I do, Andaggy, and soon I will explain it all. But tell me, have there been others who have sought the Pale God? Have there been others who have sought peace?"

"Ho!" Andaggy said, chuckling, "there have been many others. I will tell you of them.

"Among the Delawares was a great chief who was known as White Eyes, although his true name was Koquethagechton. During the war for independence, White Eyes refused to join the British in the war against the Americans. He took this pathway because he chose to be a man of peace. In your year 1778, he signed a treaty with the white fathers in Philadelphia, stating that the Delawares would not fight the Americans. In return, your leaders, including George Washington, promised White Eyes that they would establish a fourteenth state in the American Union. This state would be composed of all Indians friendly to the United States, with the Delawares at their head.

"Brother," Andaggy continued, "I was with White Eyes as his new bride when this agreement was signed, and I can tell you that not often have I seen a man filled with greater joy. White Eyes wanted his people, wanted all Indians, to be one with the white Americans, and he had done all within his power to make this so. Two months later, before the treaty could be ratified, White Eyes was murdered by a white assassin, and most of the Delaware nation went on the warpath."

"I'm sorry," I said quickly. "I did not know—"

"It is not to be worried over, my brother. My heart has long been at peace regarding him, and I shall see him soon."

For a moment I said nothing, for what could I say? She was an amazing woman, and it was as simple as that. But something which she had said surprised me greatly, for I had never heard of it before.

"A fourteenth Indian *state*?" I questioned. "I had no idea, Andaggy. I have also heard of the great Captain White Eyes, but I was told he had died of smallpox."

"And so were all others," Andaggy responded. "But I was there, and the grief in my heart speaks the truth.

"Another great man, a Delaware called Neolin, whom some called the Impostor, also declared the same message. But he lived long ago, and I know little of him.

"I would tell you, though, Malcom O'Connor, of two others who even now seek for peace. Among the Cherokee lives a woman, a beloved woman, whose name is Nan-ye-hi, Nancy Ward. She is elderly now, but always her words have been strong for peace between our peoples. I honor her name, for she has done much.

"Also, fifteen winters ago, just two years after your government first gave my people reservations, a Seneca warrior whose name is Handsome Lake beheld a mighty vision. In it three men appeared, three men who told Handsome Lake that he must give up alcohol upon pain of death. So too, they said, must all Indians. These men further told him that the practice of witchcraft, which included love magic and medicine which killed unborn babies, was evil, and he was told that the Indians must quickly return to their old way of worshipping the Peace God.

"A few weeks later, in another vision, this same Handsome Lake, whose brother is the mighty Corn Planter, was taken on a journey through the world of spirits. During this journey he met the pale god. This being told Handsome Lake that he was unhappy because so few on the land were following his religion of peace.

"Brother," Andaggy continued, "Handsome Lake's code, in which drunkenness, wanton sexual conduct, wife beating, quarreling, gambling, and warfare are outlawed, is spreading rapidly among my people. The man, as well as his brother, Chief Corn Planter, have both sent out strong voices for peace. I do what I can to further their message."

"Three men," I repeated, almost whispering. "You say that Handsome Lake saw three men in his first dream or vision?"

"Yes, brother, that is what he said."

"But so did I, Andaggy. That was my third dream! In it I too saw three men!"

"Brother," she cried, her voice filled with confusion, "I do not understand. How is it that you, a white man, can have seen these things?"

I could not answer, for truthfully I did not know. Yet in some ways I did, for the story told me by Andaggy had explained much, and a strange feeling was growing within me. However, it was not yet complete. I had not yet heard all I needed to hear. That must come before I could be certain, before I could share totally with the Indian woman.

"Andaggy," I said quietly, "I would hear the last of your story. I would hear of the death of the Peace Woman."

With her eyes the woman questioned me, begging me to stop my quest into her painful memories. Yet my desire was relentless, my need too great, and so at last, her eyes cast toward her feet, she began.

"My brother," she replied soberly, "late in the evening of Tuesday the thirteenth of December, in your year 1763, a strange thing happened in the lodge of my grandmother, where all of us made our home. I will make a telling of that."

"Mother," the small girl groaned, "there is a pain in my belly, and I do not feel well."

"Hush, my child," Tenseedaagua whispered. "It was the nuts you ate. Did you think you were a chipmunk and could store them in your cheeks? Small children do not store nuts—they eat them, and if they are greedy they get sick. You will remember this, my daughter, for one learns best when she is in pain."

The girl closed her eyes and grimaced, hoping that she could elicit a little more sympathy. When none came, she moved slowly to the pile of skins where her two younger brothers already slept.

For a time she lay in the darkness, listening to the soft snores of her father and the gentle breathing of her mother. Across the fire in the robes where her grandparents lay there was no sound, and she assumed that they too were asleep.

Outside in the night an owl made its hunger cry, and the girl shivered, giving thanks that she was not like her tiny brothers the mice. It was good to be safe and warm, for even the great pain in her stomach was not like the pain which the talons of the evil owl might bring.

Suddenly, across the fire, there was a slight movement in the bed of her grandparents. Then in the darkness she heard her grandfather's quivering voice.

"Old Woman," he said softly, "are you awake?"

Of course I'm awake, Milly scoffed, her voice a gentle whisper. *How can I sleep when*
a voice as loud as a
thousand rivers
roars into my ear,
asking me if I am
awake?

"Humph," the old man grunted, smiling into the darkness. "Your eyes may have dimmed, Old Woman, but your tongue has kept its edge well."

Both of them laughed quietly, and in the silence the old man spoke again.

"Old Woman," he said, "there is a great swelling within my heart, and I would make a telling. I would have you know that in this old heart it has always been you. Since the day of my war trail to the Huron it was you. It was you even when I could not see you except with the eyes of my spirit.

"Old Woman, it was you who has helped me to see that old things die to nourish new things, that death begins with birth, and that death is but another beginning.

"You have shown me the meaning of a flower curled up against the wind or leaning toward the sun. You have shown me the meaning of the circle of life, which is found in the sky, in the bird's nest, in the gopher hole, in the roundness of your body, and in my heart. Old Woman, in small things always there is you, as if all living things contain your thoughts. And so because of you I have learned from stones and rainbows, trees and butterflies, and even from the thunder beings, the message of peace. Old Woman, with you I have known the peace of the highest place in my heart, where good thoughts only are allowed to live. Thus now, as we prepare to travel a new path together, it is in me to awaken you and say, thank you for giving me your life."

When her grandfather grew silent there was no sound for some time, and the young girl wondered at that. At last the voice of her grandmother came softly through the darkness, and the girl thrilled with the tenderness of it.

My husband, the old woman said gently,
I give many thanks for
your words.
I . . . I . . .
When . . .
When this woman had a
great hole in
her heart,
torn open when . . . when her family was
taken from her,
you came and filled it
with love.
When this woman walked the
lonely trail
of the way of the pale god,
your footsteps were always
beside her,
lending strength.
   From her heart, then,
this old woman too sends out a
voice of thanks,
and of great love,
to you,
to . . . her husband.
With you,
she is now ready to travel the
dark road
of the end of
her life,
with joy.

In the silence which followed her grandmother's voice, the girl thought she heard the sounds of weeping. She strained to hear more, but it did not come, and so she wondered and at last fell asleep with the softness of the old ones' words still in her heart.

Hours later, in the darkness that came just before dawn, the girl awoke, filled with even greater pain. Her mother, concerned lest the others in the lodge also be awakened, took her oldest child and quietly made her way out into the trees. At a safe distance she sat down and, with a robe wrapped around both of them against the cold, she gently rocked her daughter back and forth.

Just as the light of dawn began graying the trees around them, the girl and her mother heard the terrible sounds of death coming from their bark-covered lodge. As they watched in horror from their hiding place, they saw a group of over fifty white men, armed with rifles, hatchets and rope, converge out of the forest and launch a vicious attack against the three lodges of their people.

Within minutes all who were inside were dead and scalped, and their bodies were mutilated. The lodges were set on fire, the attackers were on their horses, and they then disappeared with great shouts of triumph into the trees. Behind them they left almost half of the last surviving Susquehannocks dead.

"Brother," Andaggy continued quietly, her voice quivering with emotion, "my mother did not dare return to the bodies of her husband and her family, lest I too should be destroyed. Moving only at night she took me west to a village of the Iroquois. There I remained until I became a woman. Later I learned that two weeks following the deaths of my father, my brothers, and my grandparents, the murderers from Paxtang returned. They broke into the guardhouse in Lancaster where the fourteen remaining Susquehannocks were being kept for protection, and while a regiment of Scottish highlanders, as well as many others, looked on, these men massacred and mutilated the last of my people.

"Now," Andaggy said, with haunting finality, "I am all that is left. And though the blood of my people cries out for revenge, and though I ache with loneliness for my people, the spirit of my grandmother looks on, and in my heart I hear her voice clearly.

No, daughter of my daughter, the Peace Woman says to me,
remember the scar
engraven upon my forehead,
remember the cross
engraven on the hand of the
pale god.

Stand always in the
center of the
world,
looking outward,
and let your heart be
gentle
toward your enemies.
Teach your people to be happy,
and in the end your enemies will be
enemies only to
themselves.
Be always a seeker of peace,
be always a bearer of the
gentle heart
for such is the
true way.

"That, Malcom O'Connor, is the story of the Peace Woman. It is also why I too must strive for peace, in whatever direction I can go, and hopeless as the quest sometimes seems."

"But it is *not* hopeless," I cried. "Peace is here now. Surely you of all people must have learned that!"

Andaggy looked up, and her face broke into a radiant smile.

"Ah," she said cheerfully. "This is a wondrous thing, the way our hearts go together. Over and over this day it has happened, and it is in me to learn why. Perhaps one day I shall.

"But Malcom O'Connor, you are right. Even as I send out a voice of hopelessness, I know that such a voice is not true. Peace indeed is here, even now, even before the return of the Pale One. It is here in the hearts of those who are willing to mourn without anger or bitterness. It is here in the hearts of those who are willing to suffer without hatred. It is here in the hearts of those who are willing to serve without praise or honor. Until the gentle god of my ancestors returns, brother, peace is here, filling the hearts of those who are willing to seek it above all else. For them, and perhaps for you and for me, peace is here."

The Departure

In the emotion-packed silence which followed, I simply stared at the lovely woman who sat across the cave from me. Oh how I loved her! In the short space of one day her soul had filled my heart until I could not even speak of it, and now I loved her dearly.

As I sat looking at her I realized that my heart was singing with joy, a joy I had never before experienced, a joy I longed to tell her of. For it was over. Because of her words, my search for identity was finished, and now that I knew, I could hardly wait to tell her.

But where should I begin? I wondered. With the dream? Yes, the dream was the most important. Of all people, Andaggy deserved most to hear it, so that was where I must start. The other could come later, at any time.

"My sister," I said, my voice almost choking with excitement, "now I must speak, for what I say will ease the great sorrow which fills your heart. Now I will tell you why I risked my life to meet you here, why I have asked that you risk yours as well."

I took a deep breath and began. In hushed tones I described for the Indian woman the three men I had dreamed of. And then, gently, I told her of their message of hope, of their declaration concerning the end of despair.

The pale god was returning, I explained eagerly, and the beginning of that return was close, within a few short years. At that time life would begin to move in the direction he had taught, a happy time for those who believed, a time when they would be filled with inner peace and joy. And though it would start small, with only a very few, the word would spread at an ever-increasing rate until the whole earth would be filled with the spirit of love.

Even at this hour, I went on, not far away, the one who was to help in the return was being prepared, being given pain and sorrow so that he too might become a sincere seeker after peace. Under his inspired direction, I continued, would commence the uniting of all peoples beneath the great sacred tree of peace.

Others too were being prepared, I told her, both red and white, to hear of the higher way. Some, like myself, had been given dreams. Others would be told in different ways. Yet most, no matter how they heard of it, would embrace the way of the pale god, would follow the boy who was being prepared to lead, and would proclaim the peaceful way to others. Then, when finally all nations had heard, the pale god would at last return.

When I had finished, the Indian woman was visibly shaken.

"Do you know the name of the one who will unite peoples in preparation for the Pale One?" she asked anxiously. "Can you tell me more about him?"

I explained that I didn't know his name. But I told her of the things which I did know: his youth, his courage, and that which would become his ultimate test, the high loneliness of his mission.

"And so, Andaggy," I said quietly, "this that you have done, this that he and others will do to prepare the way for the Pale One, is not easy. Rest assured, though, that your message has been vital, for peace *will* come. It will come, and no one will have the power to stop it. Such was the word of the three men, such was the word of the Pale One who came before them. This I *know*."

"Brother," the woman said at last, her words trembling with emotion, "my voice has become weak. I am a Susquehannock woman. My grandmothers followed the way of womanhood before me. In council we have sat with our men for more generations than one can count. Yet never in our councils, not since the mysterious arrival of the pale god, have there been heard words more joyous than those you just spoke. It is in my heart to ask when the pale god of the dawn is coming, to ask who you are, to ask . . .? I would—"

Suddenly Andaggy's voice filled with concern. "Brother," she questioned, "what have you done to make certain that these powerful words are safe?"

"All I could," I said simply. Carefully then I reached back into my pack. "Everything I have learned has been written down, Andaggy. I have it here, safe in this oil-cloth wrapping. One way or another I will get it to those who need most to know of it."

The expression on Andaggy's face was something to behold. For a moment she simply stared, and then, as her eyes misted over, she reached into her own small bundle.

"Brother," she said softly, "there is *so much* that is the same between us. I too have written, in your language, all of the thoughts on peace which have filled my heart. I have also marked on paper the words of my grandmother, for I have no one to relate them to when the nights are long and the warm fire lets me know it is time for a telling. Brother, it is in me to give these words on paper to you."

When Andaggy handed the papers to me I started to protest. But the look in her eyes, a look of despair filled with pleading, tore at my heart. Doing my best to smile reassuringly, I took them.

"Andaggy," I said, as I untied my oilcloth packet, "I will keep them here, safe with my own papers. Yes, and I will protect them with my life."

Gently I folded her papers, placed them in the packet with my own, which I had most carefully prepared, retied the leather wrappings, and placed the packet back into my pack.

"My heart gives thanks," Andaggy said, "for the goodness of the Pale—"

Suddenly Andaggy's voice became still, and her entire body grew tense.

"Malcom O'Connor," she said in barely a whisper, "the American militia have found our trail. I hear them . . . . They have crossed the stream and are already much too close . . . Hurry! We must leave!"

I listened, straining, but could hear nothing save the occasional twitter of birds outside the mouth of the cave.

"But I don't—" I started to say.

"They are on the hill, near here!" she blurted, interrupting me. "We must get out, for if the Huron, the one who calls himself the Quick Killer, should see me . . . Malcom O'Connor, we *must* leave before they discover this cave, before they discover you. There is *nothing* more important than what you have told me. We must take your message—"

"No!" I said frantically. "Not yet! There is one thing more I must say—"

"Brother," Andaggy whispered fiercely, "there is no time! Now come! I will go down the hill to the south, toward the river, and draw the men after me. Once I am out of sight, you stay behind the trees and go to the east. Go to your President Madison. Tell him of your dreams. Show him our papers. Your words will mean life to all of our peoples, for they mean that we can indeed become one."

Without a backward glance, and ignoring my pleas for a moment more, Andaggy moved to the mouth of the cave, peered cautiously down into the trees, then slipped silently out into the open.

She had taken no more than three steps, however, when a rifle shot rang out from the trees above the cave. Spinning, she fell to the ground, but instantly she was back upon her feet, struggling to get even farther from the cave and from me.

Another shot rang out, and I felt my heart tear apart when I saw that Andaggy was down again. Quickly, without even thinking, I left the shelter of the cave and limped hurriedly to the side of the mortally wounded woman.

"Brother . . ." she coughed as she grasped at my arm, "I . . . I told you . . . to . . . stay back! The message! It must be taken to . . . They . . . the white men do not know of you. It is only this old woman whom they seek . . . You must . . ."

"Andaggy," I said, as I fought back the tears of emptiness and loneliness which were suddenly filling my eyes, "listen carefully, for this you must hear. Your words have moved upon my memory, and now I know. You have said that you were the last of

the Susquehannocks, but that is not so. There is another, my
sister. I *was* at the O'Connor residence when we were children.
But my name was not then Malcom O'Connor. Andaggy, though
I did not remember it until this day, I am the one who was called
Connoodaghtoh. *I* am your *brother!*"

"But . . . the massacre," she gasped. "My brother was . . . was
murdered by the Paxtang gang! They—"

"No, my sister," I said, pleading with my voice for her belief.
"When you grew ill that morning and left with our mother,
Tenseedaagua, I waited for a short time and then arose to follow.
But then the men came with their guns and their knives, and the
next thing I recall was the silence of death which was all around
me, that and the pain in my head. For two days I wandered, all
alone, and then the parents of the yellow-haired girl found me. My
older sister, until this day I did not know who I was. Now I know,
and now I know as well why it is that my heart longs so greatly for
peace."

Quickly then I tore my hat from my head and pulled back my
dark hair, which was now streaked heavily with gray.

"Andaggy," I cried, "I too carry the scar of peace upon my
forehead, the scar of a wound undeserved but well accepted. It is
the sign of our grandmother, Kyunqueagoah. It was given me by
the men from Paxtang."

"Ah, my brother . . ." Andaggy gasped, her face filled with
surprise and joy and . . . and . . . yes, it was there! Her face was
filled at last with peace. "It is good to know . . . Together we will
go forward. Together we will . . . share the message . . ."

And then, for the last time in this life, we clasped hands together. Quickly I leaned to pick her up and carry her to safety, but
at that moment my bad leg caught and buckled beneath me.
Grimacing with pain, I grabbed at it with my hands to prop it up,
succeeded in doing so, reached again for Andaggy, lifted her tiny
frame, and realized that—she was dead.

For an instant I stood numbly, holding her lifeless body tightly
against my chest. "Why?" I groaned silently. "Why now, when I
finally know . . .? Oh, my sister, I . . ."

And then into my mind came another memory, unbidden,
long forgotten, yet vivid and clear as a bright light out of the

darkest darkness. Once more I thrilled, for once more I was hearing the words of an old woman who longed for peace, an old woman who had knowingly set the course for my life those long years ago.

We were in the lodge together, and outside we could hear violent death approaching, in the form of the white men from Paxtang. Yet she thought not then of herself, but only of the tiny boy who could not find his mother. In that final moment of her life she took the time to teach again, bidding a gentle but urgent farewell to a frightened young grandson, sending out a voice to the boy who was me, filling my soul now as then with hope, with peace, with love . . .

Do not fear, I could hear her saying,
for we are going to a
happy place.
　　From my youth
I have dreamed very often,
and in my dream I see always a
place of
light,
where the grass is more
green than
green,
where the roof of the
sky
is more blue than
an old woman can say,
and where the tree of peace
bears fruit in the center of
the village of the
world.
There dwells the Pale One
of the gentle heart,
the god of peace.
There too this old woman longs to dwell,
in peace,
with those she loves,
forever.

Take hold of this old hand,
my son,
stand with me,
and—

Barooom!

Epilogue

"Sam!" a voice called softly into the stillness of the early evening air. "Can't tell for certain with all this powder smoke, but I think you got both of them."

"It weren't me," Sam replied. "I never shot. I never even saw anybody. Did any of you boys fire your weapons?"

From the trees there came a chorus of negative responses.

"Then it must have been the Huron," Sam growled. "I wonder how—?"

"Huron?" the colonel bellowed. "I never gave the order for him to fire! I . . . Say, where *is* the Huron?"

For a moment there was silence, and then a voice called out of the trees.

"He's not where he was, colonel. He's gone. Vanished."

"But how could that be, Aaron? I didn't give the order to—"

"Colonel!" a young voice called.

"What is it, son?"

"Colonel, I didn't mean to do it, but I . . . I fired too. I hurried to keep up with the Huron, saw the Iroquois spy, heard the

Huron's shot, and when he fired, my musket seemed to go off by itself. I don't even remember pulling the trigger."

"Happened to me once too," Sam interjected. "That ain't too unusual."

"And to me," another added. "I didn't even know my musket had fired."

"But colonel," Sam added, "that there's still only two shots. There were three fired."

"You're right, Sam. All right, men! Who fired the third shot?"

Again there was silence, and again Aaron's voice, from back in the trees, gave the answer.

"It was the Huron, sir. I'd know the sound of his rifle anyplace. He fired twice."

"Twice, eh?" the colonel said, surprised. "That's right fast shooting, especially for an Indian. Still, I didn't give the order to fire, and . . . Oh, well, I suppose there was no harm done. After all, they're only Indians, the whole bunch of them. Nothing to worry about.

"Say, lad, get on up there and make sure they're dead. Take their scalps too if you're of a mind to. Since the Huron's gone, I suppose they should be yours."

There was a brief scuffle in the bushes, and then the wiry form of a young man entered the clearing and advanced cautiously toward the two still bodies.

"Colonel," he said, his voice strained and curiously high-pitched. "We got 'em! We . . . They're both dead, and . . . and . . . Wait a minute! I . . . I . . . Oh, no!"

There was a strange cry from the young man's throat, and the colonel called out in alarm.

"Son? What is it, lad?"

"Colonel," the young man cried, his voice choked with emotion. "This Indian's a . . . a woman! An *old woman*! And the man with her, the other one? I *know* him! He's white, and he's old too! Colonel, we've gone and murdered some elderly people! *I've* killed my father's—"

"Whoa, there!" the colonel shouted angrily, breaking the boy off. "Take it easy, son. Nobody's murdered anybody. Do you hear me?"

The lad, still alone in the clearing with the two bodies, stared off down the hill in shocked disbelief. "But, sir," he called quickly, "you don't under—"

"That's enough!" the colonel shouted out. "Don't question your superior officer, boy! And don't worry. I understand well enough, and so will you when you get older. Killing isn't killing when you're killing enemies! Why, I recall a time when . . ."

The young man, sick at heart, weeping openly, and suddenly wishing more than ever that he had never quarreled with his father, turned away from the droning voice of the colonel, laid aside his rifle, and knelt down beside the two slain people.

"I . . . I'm sorry," he whispered, sobbing quietly. Slowly he placed his hands on both the old woman's arm and the hand of the man who had fallen beneath her, the man who had been his father's friend, the man who had so wanted peace.

"I didn't mean to . . . to kill anyone," he pleaded through his tears, hoping somehow that they would hear. "Honestly I didn't! And I swear that I will never kill again. *Never!*

"And sir," he continued, looking down into the pain-filled face of the old man whose name had been Malcom O'Connor, "somehow I will learn the way of peace. I swear it! I don't know how, but somehow, some way, I will make up for . . . for this that I have done! That is a promise!"

For a moment the young man wiped at his eyes, and then an early evening breeze, brushing past him, lifted a strand of the woman's hair and tossed it haphazardly across her face. As the boy unconsciously reached to straighten it, he saw the old man's eyes suddenly flicker open, and he pulled quickly back.

"S . . . Sir," the lad stammered, "M . . . Mister O'Connor, I . . . I . . . didn't—"

"Son," the old man whispered, his voice sounding tired and distant, "don't . . . don't fret yourself. For me . . . and for my . . . sister, it is as . . . it should be. We have sought . . . peace . . . and now . . . at last we . . . we have . . . found it."

"No!" the boy shouted, his voice filled with fear. "Don't say that! I'll get you to a doctor! I'll get—"

"My son, there . . . is no . . . need. For us . . . each of us . . . this is past. But for you . . . for you . . ."

The man was wracked by a sudden fit of coughing, and the boy knelt helplessly by, holding the old man's head in his arms and wishing with all his heart that his father was there.

"Son," the man gasped, fighting now for each ragged breath, ". . . in my pack . . . papers . . . the tidings of . . . peace . . . for you to . . ."

The old man coughed again, his eyes squeezed tight against the pain, and the boy felt his own chest tightening with fear and concern. The old man must not die! He must not! But what could he do? he asked himself. What could he possibly to to help?

The man's lips were moving once more, almost silently, and the boy leaned forward, straining to hear.

". . . mark . . . undeserved but well accepted . . . is yours. Our deaths at your hands . . . give . . . give it . . . to you. The papers . . . you must now carry . . . forward . . . with peace . . . peace . . ."

The man's eyes flickered open once more, he looked into the face of the boy, and a radiant smile burst like a sunrise across his tired and ragged features. For a moment the smile held, glowing, peaceful, forgiving—yes, forgiving! And then slowly the man's face relaxed, the light of joy faded from his eyes, and he was gone.

For long seconds the boy knelt silently, his tears falling unheeded onto the still forms beneath him. He had killed! Through some terrible mistake, with the beautiful new rifle which his father had given him, the rifle which had been meant only for good, he had killed. He had murdered this old man, this kindly old gentleman who had so desperately wanted peace. Now the man was dead, and there was no one left to carry on his work.

Now the boy's eye caught sight of something protruding from the old man's pack. After a moment's hesitation he pulled it free, realizing as he did so that it was the sheaf of papers of which the old man had spoken, wrapped carefully in an oilcloth packet.

The boy's first thought was to report his find to the colonel. But then, suddenly, he knew he wouldn't. Not ever! The colonel would not understand, for he was the kind of man who could never understand the things which the boy felt certain those papers contained. Somehow the colonel's heart was not right for understanding. Nor, most likely, would it ever be.

Thrusting the packet quickly beneath his waistcoat, the boy who had now become a man stood, saluted the two still forms smartly, and once again wiped at his eyes.

"Peace will come!" he whispered again as he did his best to smile. "Someday I will help peace to come! You have my word on it!"

Turning quickly away, and purposely leaving his new rifle where it lay, the young man whose eyes and heart were now old with understanding gradually became aware once more of the distant voice of his commander.

". . . and that is why I say they deserved to die. We didn't know who they were, or that they were white and female. Besides, they no doubt deserved what they got. You yourself saw they were scheming something together, something obviously evil. It must have been. Otherwise, why would they have hidden from us? All those Indians and Indian-lovers are alike, you understand, men *or* women! Just goes to show you, son, how justice always wins out. One way or the other, by thunder, we'll force these redskinned murderers to be peaceful."

He paused only briefly. "All right, men. Back to the horses! This has been a long day. Let's get home before that cow of Aaron's drops her calf."

There was a brief flurry of movement. The young man took one more heartsick but determined look backward, touched the packet beneath his waistcoat to reassure himself, smiled through his tears with a renewed sense of hope, and urged his horse forward into the twilight of the warm spring evening. It was time, he suddenly understood, that he was going home, for that was where peace must start.